HEAD GAMES

HEAD GAMES
CRAIG MCDONALD

BLEAK HOUSE BOOKS

MADISON | WISCONSIN

Published by Bleak House Books,
an imprint of Big Earth Publishing
923 Williamson St.
Madison, WI 53703

ISBN 13 (cloth): 978-1-932557-42-8

Library of Congress Cataloging-in-Publication Data has been applied for.

Printed in the United States of America

11 10 09 08 07   1 2 3 4 5 6 7 8 9 10

Set in Minion Pro

Cover and Book Design by
Von Bliss Design — "Book Design By Bookish People"
http://www.vonbliss.com

This novel is for
Tom Russell & Andrew Hardin
for supplying the soundtrack.

Dedicated to the memory of William Charles Sipe, Sr.

The strong men keep coming on,
They go down shot, hanged, sick, broken.
They live on fighting.
— Carl Sandburg

Fifty years ago a man could go to Mexico or Central America and take his pick of a dozen wars, insurrections or marauding expeditions. But the rules changed and soldiers of fortune have to admit that free-lance fighting is a thing of the past. The world has gone to hell.
— Emil L. Holmdahl

Rakish in his eye patch. Pundit when sane …
A reminder: men were men then.
— James Ellroy

Dead or alive.
— George W. Bush

BOOK ONE

1957:
THE
LAND OF HOPE
AND DREAMS

01

WE were sitting in a back room of a cantina on the outskirts of Ciudad Juárez, three drinks in, when Bill Wade reached into the dusty duffel bag he had tucked under our table and plunked down the Mexican general's head.

The skull was wrapped in a Navajo rug. A few patches of mummified flesh clung to the ivory- and caramel-colored bone. Some moustache hair was stubbornly hanging in there. Could have been any Indian's/Mexican's skull—but for that too-recognizable, too-prognathic jawbone. That famous underbite trumped any of *my* doubts.

I took a swig of bad tequila, winced, and reached across the table, flipping the corners of the Indian rug up and over the severed head.

"For Christ's sake," said Bud Fiske, the too-young poet sent to interview me, "stow that thing, won't you?"

Wade glanced at Fiske and then back at me. I nodded and said, "Bud is right. Get the head the hell back in that bag, you crazy bastard."

Old Wade frowned and bundled up the bandit's skull. He shoved the head back into the duffel bag, then took a shot of whiskey. He shook his own head, pouting. "Jesus Christ, Hector," he said, "I could use your help with this thing. There's real money to be had here. Thought you'd understand, if anyone would."

Long memories and thick wallets: *Oh, I understand 'em.*

"I get it, Wade," I said. "But I also know you don't sit on this side of the border, flaunting the stolen skull of General Francisco fucking Villa—even behind closed doors."

Wade: color him one reckless, wall-eyed cocksucker.

The bandit had been dead for decades. It was something like thirty years since Villa was gunned down leaving a wedding. Yet you could impale Pancho Villa's rotting skull on a pike and drive through El Paso, or, especially, through Columbus, New Mexico, and find yourself cheered as a hero.

But dare to display that skull on the south side of the borderlands? Well, that was something akin to suicide.

South of the border, they crucified people on still-standing telegraph poles.

They'd slice off the bottoms of your feet and set you out a few miles in the desert.

Or, in the rainy season, maybe they'd just stake you out over a spiky maguey plant. Those suckers are hard and sharp and they grow several inches in the night. There is no other term for it but "dusk-to-dawn impalement."

But now the bandit's skull sat under our table between the feet of Eskin "Bud" Fiske, aspiring, myopic poet and my latest would-be interviewer; Bill Wade, drunkard, soldier-of-fortune and con man; and me, Hector Lassiter, pulp-writer-turned-crime-writer, turned-lately-screenwriter.

Bud Fiske, this jug-eared, scrawny kid, had been flown down to New Mexico by *True* to profile me. For four days or thereabouts, he had dogged my heels as drinking companion, sometimes driver, coat-holder and maybe half-assed worthy Boswell.

Wade was a twenty-year fugitive up north. Wade heard word I'd crossed the bridge again. He knew all of my favorite hotels and bordellos on the south side of the border. He found me easily enough.

Wade had this proposition.

So I bit—mostly just to give young Bud something for his article other than samples of my lavish boozing, brawling and whoring.

I never saw Pancho's head coming, though.

The waitress brought Wade another watered-down whiskey—he was rationing himself. She frowned at me. I'd known her for maybe thirty years. She used to be something to look at. In her prime, she inspired at least half-a-dozen folk songs, cowboy ballads and *corridos*. But in the last fifteen years every *vaquero* and fruit picker in a fifty-mile radius had had her at least twice. Her black hair was streaked with gray and she was missing an important tooth. Faleena banged down Wade's drink and limped out, slamming the door behind her, closing out the music from the bar—"Volver, Volver," I think. I shook my head at the waitress' exit, then glared at Wade. If she'd come in when that severed head was sitting on our table…

Through the back window, I heard low moans; cries of feral cats screwing in the dark; the *grita* of some old Mexican woman, chilled by *something*.

I heard something else, too—something that sounded a bit like a shotgun being prepped.

Or maybe not.

It was outside, anyway.

Wade slammed his shot of whiskey. He belched, then said, "Prescott still wants the skull, Hector."

"Prescott" would be Prescott Bush, current United States Senator and the bastard alleged to have engineered the theft of Pancho Villa's head.

Here's a capsule history from your hack writer:

1878: Doroteo Arango was born in Durango, Mexico.

1895: Doroteo's sister was raped. Her brother killed her attacker and became a fugitive.

Five or six years later, Arango rechristened himself "Pancho Villa" and became a Robin Hood-like hero to the Mexican poor, and an eventual revolutionary.

To this day, Villa remains a kind of hero of mine.

Indeed, "General" Villa was an American media darling—for a time.

In 1913, Black Jack Pershing was sent down south to take Pancho's measure. There's a famous photo of the two standing together at Fort Bliss, beaming. Over one of Villa's shoulders, you get a glimpse of Rodolfo Fierro—one world-class sociopath and first-rate cocksucker. He hastened Pancho's fall from grace.

But I get ahead of myself.

The Wilson administration, for reasons that at best remain stupefying, eventually elected to piss all over Villa. (The bastards had already executed Emiliano Zapata. "It is better," Zapata said, "to die on your feet than to live on your knees.")

In 1915, Woodrow Wilson and company crawled in bed with Venustiano Carranza.

I'm a crime writer, so please trust me on this: you do not want to do business with any man who wears blue-tinted lenses and answers to the name "Venustiano."

Villa famously took his American rejection very badly.

Pancho was right to do so.

But just how badly he took that rejection remains a mystery that shapes history to this day.

Maybe—just *maybe*—Pancho shrugged it off.

But the so-called "nattering nabobs of negativity" will try to convince you otherwise. They'll make a case that Pancho Villa made the first and only successful foreign military attack against the United States mainland.

I could never make myself believe that Francisco Villa personally raided New Mexico in March of 1916 and killed all those folks in Columbus.

But the slaughter of all those American civilians by whomever?

Well, that triggered the "Punitive Expedition," which I was, shamefacedly, a party to—a callow kid who caught a growth spurt and lied about his age. They sent Jack Pershing back into Mexico within days of the attack on Columbus, this time to take Villa, "dead or alive."

Okay: *yeah*, sure—I rode behind Black Jack Pershing.

Sure, I reluctantly chased Pancho's shadow through the Mexican desert for nearly a year before that pinched-faced politician Woodrow Wilson shut down the show in February 1917 and shipped us over to Europe to be cannon fodder and trench filler.

Here's the thing—crusades change.

The year was 1923: Long retired and gone to fat, Pancho Villa was gunned down by unknown assassins. Just his continued living, even peacefully, was a presumed threat to someone. Many claim President Warren G. Harding sent a hired gun down to Mexico to take Villa out. Something about oil and American business holdings. Rings true.

Pancho Villa's last recorded words: "Don't let it end like this …
tell them I said *something*."

But that was all that the poor bastard said.

In February 1926, Pancho's grave was robbed and his head was
chopped off.

A fabled unfound treasure of Villa's and his missing head became linked in folklore and Tex-Mex myth.

Some claim a map was hidden inside Pancho's stolen skull.
Others claim that a map was tattooed on Villa's rotting scalp.

In theory, hell, either could be true.

But there were other myths attached to Pancho's head.

They actually arrested two men for stealing the general's nev-
er-recovered skull—Emil Holmdahl and a fella name of Alberto
Corral. Holmdahl told the *federales* the skull was already on its
way back to Columbus, New Mexico … maybe as some kind of
morbid recompense.

I vaguely knew Holmdahl way back then. He was an alleged
spy, a mercenary, a fleeting captain in Villa's army. But Holmdahl
was a turncoat flavor of cocksucker and he'd soon enough flipped
sides to serve as a paid guide for Black Jack and the rest of us in
our 1916 hunt for Villa.

Men shouldn't turn on men that way. Fight alongside a man
and then take money to hunt him? That notion goes down hard
and thick with me.

Lean and prematurely white-haired, Emil was more than a little reminiscent of that pussy-whipped communist Dash Hammett,
my equally treacherous old *Black Mask Magazine* stablemate.

Holmdahl allegedly stole the skull for Prescott Bush, who purportedly wanted the head to use for dark rituals undertaken by
Yale's Skull and Bones Society. They say that many years before,

Prescott personally stole Geronimo's skull for more of the Skull and Bones' satanic shenanigans.

Senator Bush was said to have paid evil Emil twenty-five grand to pillage Pancho's grave in Panteon de Dolores.

True or not, Villa's head remained, at least officially, *lost*.

"Inflation being what it is, he'll now pay eighty grand for the skull," Wade said. "I'll give you half. All you have to do is take it back across the border with you. Bush will have train tickets waiting. First class. You just take the skull on up to Connecticut and personally turn it over to Senator Bush. 'Cause, you know, I can't go back … if the bastards ever got their hands on me …"

Heh. Very tempting. It would likely be a lark.

And, if Bud Fiske could be persuaded not to get too detailed in terms of the eventual recipient of the skull—and the skull's true identity? Well, what a hell of a profile *True* would have from young Bud. His resulting article could enhance my already bloated legend as a hell-raising hack writer.

But I played coy … just trying to keep myself interested. It was a harder task every year, as—as a wise man said—"the ground pulled harder" at me.

I sat back in my chair and laced my fingers across my chest. I contemplated the bullfighter's cape and crossed picador's sharp-ended *banderillas* mounted on the wall between flanking *castoreños*.

"Hell, I dunno." As I said this I glanced over at young Bud. My kid poet was sitting there breathless—half-fascinated, half-sickened by what he might become a party to—this dark deal threatening to enfold him. "Me and Bud, we've gotta get ourselves out to California, Wade. I have a meeting with Orson Welles about a script gig. I'm already running behind schedule. And getting that rotting sucker across the border, Wade? Well, 'half' seems hardly fair. Hardly seems commensurate to the risk."

Bill Wade leaned across the table, face and ears red. "Jesus, Hector, why don't you pull that famous old Peacemaker of yours and just rob me outright, you son of a bitch."

I smiled and tipped my chair down on all four legs. I slapped his beefy arm (poor bastard was running to middle-aged flab.) "Naw, Wade. Half is actually more than generous. I was just having some sport. How did poor Prescott lose Pancho's head first time around? I thought—"

Crash!

The door slammed open—suddenly hanging half off its hinges. Four *federales* crowded through. Each of the soldiers was toting a shotgun. Pretty clearly, they aimed—really aimed—to shoot first. Shotgun slaughter.

Wade was an old campaigner—a seasoned soldier of fortune who could take care of himself. So I reached out to push young Fiske to the floor. But Bud, bless him, was already moving. I tipped over our table, crouched low behind it and whipped out my Colt '73 Peacemaker.

The first shotgun blast vaporized roughly half my cover—splinters of wood peppered my legs and left arm.

Sometimes, in the fog of attack, you don't have the luxury of decision: you're hit, and you swing back—half-blind and enraged. Sometimes, in that white rage, you don't swing wisely.

I fired twice. The tunic of one of the *federales* blossomed red. He collapsed, falling back against one of his partners, fouling that fucker's shot. *Christ.* Found myself another axiom: *When you murder a federale, you know you're fully committed.*

Wade broke his chair across the face of another of the feds. The chair was hewn from mesquite wood—really tough stuff—maybe more than enough to kill the bastard. Wade was reaching for his piece when one of the two *federales* still standing raised his shotgun and rendered poor Wade every bit as headless as Pancho Villa.

I slew Wade's slayer with a single shot between the eyes.

The last of the *federales* was drawing a bead on me. It was looking like lights-out time for Hector Mason Lassiter.

But then the Mexican's arms flew back, spastic-like. The shotgun flew as the *federale* fell to the floor. Bud Fiske, my poet/Boswell, had grabbed one of the picador's spikes from the wall and driven that wicked stick into the Mexican officer's right eye—straight on through and right out the back.

I patted down what was left of Wade. I grabbed car keys, wallet, a small notebook and Wade's chrome-plated .45. I scooped up the duffel bag and said, "Follow me, kid."

We crashed through the back window, duffel bag first to take the dusty glass. Bud was hard on my heels, toting the impaled *federale's* shotgun. I sent him back in for my half-empty tequila bottle.

02

THE night air was like a tonsil-teasing soul kiss—the rare scent of desert rain carried on the wind and heat lightning roaming the horizon.

Bill Wade's wheels were easy enough to spot. Wade had always favored Mercurys. But it had been a long time since he could cross the border for a replacement. This one was a vintage '49 Merc, low-slung and pimp purple with red and white candy-stripe upholstery. I checked the glove compartment and thrust my arms under the front and back seats, groping. Bud stood there wide-eyed, knees shaking and teeth chattering.

I popped the trunk and found two identical duffel bags—dead ringers for the one I'd carried from the cantina. I indulged a hunch and grabbed both bags, gathering them up with the third and stowing them in the backseat of my '57 Bel Air.

Bud was standing there, shivering. It wasn't that cold yet. I placed my callused hands on his sloped and bony shoulders and squeezed. I searched his scared eyes and felt bad for what I saw.

I smiled and said, "First man you ever put down, son?" I hedged, "Not to say he was necessarily dead, Bud."

Fiske's eyes were skittish. He said, "First I'm pretty sure of."

I smiled and patted his cheek. "Some compelling ambiguity in your phrasing there, scribe of mine. Just like all good writers. Fair enough. You had my back, son. Saved my life. I won't forget that, Bud. If you'd done anything else, or if you'd done nothing, I'd be dead right now. Sometimes we don't have the luxury of choosing the fights we can win, son—the fights find us, win or lose. So you fight like hell to stay alive. Instinct. Don't let it eat at you."

Bud was wearing a black tie emblazoned with a busty slut casting a pair of dice. Sucker was swanky. Hated like hell to do it, but there was nothing else for it. I loosened the knot, grabbed the fat end and tugged.

Bud said, "What are you doing?"

I relieved him of the half-empty tequila bottle and wadded in his tie. Now Bud was looking freshly concerned. Fishing my sports jacket's pocket for my Zippo, I said, "*Federales* tend to travel in fifties, Bud. We sorely need a distraction … and a scorched-earth trail, I think." I flicked the Zippo open one-handed, right to left, nice and slick. I touched off the dice-throwing lady's big breasts, opened the door of Wade's Mercury and cast the bottle at the dash.

There was this big *whoosh!* And it was *adios* to Wade's sweet ride.

I took the shotgun from Bud, shouldered it and took aim. I put one barrel to the front license plate and another to the back, just to make sure there'd be no tracing of plates. I tossed the shotgun into the smoldering front seat.

I clapped my interviewer's arm. "C'mon Bud, before she blows." I tossed him the keys to my Chevy. "You drive, son … it'll help take your mind off the bedlam." I didn't volunteer the rest—lately, my night vision was inexplicably poor.

As Bud drove us north, I checked the spare duffel bags. Two more skulls—but these lacked that telltale underbite.

Canards.

Clearly, Wade was playing some marks … some Pancho-Villa-head version of three-card monte, maybe.

The light was too dim for me to check the notebook for clues to the identities of Wade's intended pigeons.

The compartment of my Chevy flashed with orange light. The Mercury's gas tank must have blown.

Bud split his attention between me and the dusty one-lane trailing on up toward the border. "That waitress, the one with the limp," he said, "I kinda sensed you two have a history. Will she finger you?"

I pushed a button on the dash and the ragtop roof released and commenced its retreat behind the backseat. The desert air was cool across our faces. Could really smell the rain on the wind now. I growled over the wind sheer, "You're sharp, kiddo. Got a good eye on you and that's a necessary writer's trait. Faleena's served me for thirty years, at least—longer than you've been around. Served me drinks and more—when she was still pretty—as you've probably surmised. But she doesn't know my real name. So there's no sweat there, kiddo."

"How do you think those soldiers knew to look for Wade and the head?"

"Well, Bud, that is troubling. That one's got even me wondering. But Wade was an alcoholic. Maybe, in his cups, he talked to the wrong son of a bitch. But there's another possibility. Prescott Bush, the senator up north? He's got himself a lot of ties to U.S. intelligence … could easily enough divine Wade's unhappy situation—I mean the federal warrant out on Wade. Bush would learn easy enough—particularly after Wade made contact—where to look for him. Why pay eighty grand for something this hot when you can just take it?"

"What about the border? We gotta get back across."

I winked at Fiske. It was vintage me—cocky and awash in blarney. "Well, I'm not sweating that and neither should you, Bud," I said. "The Mex cops will be a few hours sorting out that mess at the cantina. We'll be across the bridge by then, back where they can't fuck with tough gringos like thee and me."

Bud shook his head, palpably dubious. So call my poet/interviewer smart, too. I shook loose a Pall Mall and fired it up. I'd yet to see Fiske smoke, but said, "You want one, son?"

Bud nodded, grateful. "Hell yeah." I passed him mine and lit another. God bless the windproof technology of those geniuses at Zippo—suckers were doing hero's work.

Bud suppressed a cough, then blew smoke from the right side of his mouth. He asked, "That really Pancho Villa's head?"

"Pretty sure it is."

"I remember in my research for your bio reading that you chased Villa with General Pershing, so I guess you'd know. Those other bags—what's in 'em?"

"More heads."

"Jesus Christ."

"Yeah, Wade was a schemin', me thinks."

I checked our dust. There was a guttering glow back there. We were probably too far away for the light to be coming from the burning Mercury. But it might be nothing. All the same, I reloaded my Colt.

Bud said, "Trouble, Hector?"

"Naw, Bud. Just being like a good Boy Scout."

That light behind us was vibing menace—and getting closer.

But so was the border.

Bud kept fretting. I fiddled with the radio. President Eisenhower was going on about something regarding a high school in the old South. Like most, I liked Ike—but not at this hour. So I found some mariachi music and cranked it up loud.

Just for kicks, to lighten the mood, like Pancho Villa fleeing Columbus, New Mexico, I whooped like some Apache whose blood was up and fired a single shot in the air.

With any luck, maybe the falling bullet would kill the bastard driving the car I was fairly certain was following us.

03

THE border agent was one weary-assed wage-slave. It was all routine and rote with this fella. He asked, "Anything to declare?"

My back was pressed to the passenger seat door and my legs stretched out and crossed at the ankles. I smiled and hoisted the duffel bag. "Just the head of Pancho Villa." I blew two perfect smoke rings.

The agent snorted and smiled. "Good one, Slick. Second time I've heard that one this shift. Hope you didn't bring back the spic clap with the bandit's head." He waved us through.

Bud Fiske said, "Where to, chief?"

"My place." I smiled and reached across and feinted one at his chin. "We're in my country now, Bud. Feel free to put your foot to the firewall."

* * *

I rarely returned home during that time. There were too many wicked-bad memories crowding my too-empty, haunted house. I

had the cash—paperback reprint royalties, movie money, cock-
and bullfighting winnings—so it was a lot of hotel time for me in
those days. But I held onto the hacienda, unable to let go even if I
couldn't sleep in it anymore. It remained a beautiful old place—a
posh pad in La Mesilla; two stories of stucco with a wrap-around
second-floor porch, hard by the Rio Grande.

We rolled up the crushed-oyster-shell driveway; Bud was still
at the wheel. I handed Wade's chrome .45 butt-first to my latest
interviewer. Bud looked at it, then thrust the rod down his pants.
"Expecting more trouble, Hector?"

"Just being careful, Bud." I checked the matching bags, looking for the head with the profound underbite. I popped the trunk,
lugged out the spare tire, and dropped the bag with the real bandit's
head into the wheel well. I rolled the spare tire out of sight behind
a stand of cottonwood. Bud slammed shut the trunk. I handed him
one of the two remaining duffels. He handled it just like what it
was—a bag containing a severed human head.

I keyed us in and stashed my duffel in the coat closet. Bud
flipped on some lights, then whistled low. "Beautiful," he said.

Bud trailed me through the house to my study. The walls were
lined with books. One wall was filled with my various first editions
and translations—French, Spanish, even one in fucking Yiddish.
I sometimes wonder how much of what I wrote remains in those
non-English versions. How do killers and rats and whores and private dicks "travel" in the Romance languages? But the French seem
to love me, just the same. Those suckers have always gotten noir.

I took the third duffel from my interviewer and deposited it
behind the leather couch by the fireplace.

Bud zeroed in on the oil paintings over the bar. One was of
Dolores, my daughter who never saw four; the other was of her
mother, Maria. Both were about a year dead ... Dolores a bit lon-

ger. I'd sensed Bud had heard some of the wicked rumors, that he was burning to ask me about my girls. Fortunately for him, he'd had the good sense these past few days not to press. But I knew for sure that he had heard the whispers when he pointed at my daughter—and just my daughter—and said again, "Beautiful."

I met his gaze, bit my lip and nodded. "Thanks," I said. Bud got my unstated message: *Don't you dare go further.* I slipped behind the bar and fetched a couple of big tumblers. "Like the man said," I said, "'You've got to find what you love and let it kill you.' So we drink it neat here, Bud Fiske. What's your poison, *hombre*?"

"I'd kill—die—for a Scotch," the young poet said.

"Blended or single malt?"

"God, single malt if you've got it."

"Good man." I broke a seal on a fresh bottle of Talisker and poured four fingers apiece. We tapped glasses and hissed together at the burn. I topped off our glasses and said, "Now my faithful Indian companion, we look this over." I slipped Bill Wade's notebook from my blazer's breast pocket and tore it in half. I passed the back half to Bud and started flipping through the remaining portion. I squinted. It was suddenly hard to focus. I moved the notepad back and forth, trying to find a range where I could read it. Bud frowned. "When was the last time you ate?"

"Maybe noon."

"Blood sugar. You should have your sugar checked; you may be toeing up to diabetes."

Toeing. Good one. My feet had certainly been hurting enough in recent months. *Great.*

Bud set off in search of my kitchen. "See if I can find something for you to eat," he said over his shoulder. "That'll help."

Yeah, I thought, *good luck finding anything*. I had fired the help six months before—probably the last time any grocery shopping was done.

I dug around in my desk's center drawer and found a magnifying glass. Like some dipsomaniacal/diabetic Sherlock Holmes, I started scanning pages covered in Wade's cramped handwriting. There were a couple of longish entries on Emil L. Holmdahl, the alleged head thief. Seemed the sucker was maybe still north of the turf. That could be good, or it could be bad. Holmdahl's last known whereabouts: Van Nuys, California.

There were longish notes on some Yale fraternities—not the Skull and Bones Society, but some Greek outfits.

I retrieved the half of the notebook I'd handed Bud and looked it over. There were several pages covered with notes regarding something called the "Wednesday Group"—some organization based in El Paso.

I heard breaking glass.

I stowed the notebook's halves under the bar and slipped out my Colt, headed for the kitchen. I didn't quite make the door of my study when Bud flew through, propelled face first.

Three shotgun-toting young guys—roughly Bud's own age—followed him in. All three leveled their shotguns at my crotch.

Nodding, I slowly put my Colt down on the bar. Then I raised my hands.

04

THE intruders sure weren't toughs.

Hell, they looked like college kids who had raided their dilettante daddies' gun cabinets.

I've been on the wrong end of more guns than a man has a right to face and remain standing. But you learn some things, staring down the iron at all the eyes of those that have you in their bead.

You just maybe get good at judging.

These young clowns were strictly sad amateur hour, I decided. They wouldn't shoot us. But they sure could be clumsy—or easily spooked. I carefully bent down to help Bud to his feet. I was relieved to see that they'd stripped Fiske of Wade's .45. I looked at Bud and whispered, "Follow my lead. No goddamned heroics this time, son."

One of the trio was wearing a sweater vest and a bow tie. Two others were wearing jackets emblazoned with Greek letters. I smiled, pointed, and said, "Yale, Class of …?"

One slick winked and tipped his shotgun barrel up against his shoulder, casual-like, as though he was standing sentry at the fraternity house. He had blond hair and world class dimples. He smirked and said, "Class of '59."

Bud sneered back and droaned, fairy-like, "Oh, go *Har*vard."

"Easy," I said to Fiske. I moved to the bar, hands again up, and retrieved my drink. I handed the other glass to Bud. I took a swig and said, "You fellas follow us all the way from Ciudad Juárez?"

Blondie smiled. "Wasn't too hard."

I shrugged and waved a hand. "Well, we didn't try to make it hard, old son. Though I'm shocked you got out of the cantina with pointdexter there in his sweater vest and bow tie. *Chee-rist* on a crutch ..."

The scrawny, bow-tied fucker's ears surged red and his feet shifted nervously. I had this epiphany: he might actually be provoked to shoot me. So it was change-up time. "You lads working for Prescott Bush?"

Blondie again: "Hell no. He's old Skull and Bones Society. They've been after Villa's head forever. We're Sigma Chi. It'll send those S&Bs over the edge when they learn we've got Villa's head. And now we get that sucker for free. The dead geezer back in taco land was gonna charge us one thousand dollars for Villa's skull. But we'll just take it from you. Now where is it?"

Bud's started getting into it again. "Don't do it Hector. They're all bluff. 'Specially bow tie there. Fuckin' pillow-biter, I 'spect."

I had furnishings to think about. And I was getting kind of fond of Bud. As bow tie raised his shotgun, pointing it at my interviewer, I stepped between them. "Naw boys, easy now." I looked back over my shoulder. "Ain't worth it, Bud. Win some, lose some. Stand down, Fiske—I mean that, goddamn it."

I jerked my head in the direction of the leather sofa. "The head is in the duffel bag, behind the couch. Take it and get your frat asses out of my house."

Blondie hurdled over my couch like the track star he probably was. He balanced the bag on the back of the couch, opened it and looked inside. He surely tried to put himself across as some kind of hard case, but I could see him swallowing hard, breathing through his mouth, trying to keep himself from puking all over the mummified head. "It's jake," he squeaked out in a girl's voice. "Let's roll, boys."

The trio backed out. The pointdexter, the last out the door, hollered, "Sigma Chi forever, you fucking assholes!"

I laughed and raised my drink and said, "Go, Sigs." I took a big gulp of single malt. Ah, whiskey—the milk of short-term mercy.

The front door slammed, then tires squealed in the night.

Bud and I were into our second round of single malt when I heard the door open again.

It was four more college boys. These boys carried baseball bats. I didn't even stand up; just gestured with my drink and arched an eyebrow. I said, "Zeta Psi?"

The biggest one—a footballer probably, maybe a linebacker— said, "Hell no: Delta Kappa Epsilon."

"Terrific," I growled. "Don't break anything. It's in a bag in the hall closet, by the front door. Stick it to those Skull and Boners for Hector Lassiter." I toasted their backs.

More squealing tires. This time I struggled up. I pulled my car into the garage and locked it down. I doused the lights and double-bolted the front door. Place looked abandoned again. We retreated to my windowless library.

Bud brought me a plate of crackers smeared with tuna fish, mayonnaise and diced pickles and a bowl of tomato soup. He had recovered his new .45 and shoved that sucker back down his pants. "What now, Hector? What do we do with that real head?"

I chewed, talking through my food. "First thing? Push that rod a few inches left. You don't want it to accidentally discharge and blow off your cock. That said, there's eighty grand to be made here, Bud. Maybe more, bard of mine. I'm having a hard time ignoring that. How about you? You in?"

"Gotta make all that back across the border matter for something, I guess," young Fiske said. It was false bravado—he was visibly shaken from having killed that *federale*. But I loved him for his bluster. Bud said, "Forty grand might do the trick." He was shaping up to be a good lad.

"Then, Bud," I said, "I say we finish this bottle. Then we get some shovels and we head toward Orogrande. There's an old Mex cemetery down there. Migrant farmworkers killed by some long-ago twister, circa 1926. Makes 'em roughly the right vintage. We're suddenly runnin' low on spare skulls. Attrition rate is too fuckin' high tonight, and God only knows how many fraternities are angling for Pancho's head. So I'm thinkin' we need a refill. And I think we should be properly drunk in order to see to those dark needs."

I checked Bud's haunted eyes. He was hangin' in there … even looked game for it. My kind of poet.

05

WE were a quarter mile from *casa de Lassiter* when the stench of burning rubber reached us. There was a strange glow on the horizon. We drew closer and saw black, spiraling plumes of smoke.

It was a car fire—a ragtop something with its top down.

The side panel of the burning car was riddled with bullet holes—like someone strafed it to blow out the tires and kill the driver, get the car stopped. Three flaming bodies remained inside. Three smoking mouths were opened wide in final agony.

A too-familiar and now-empty duffel bag had been discarded on the roadside. I moved around to the back of the car and peered through the flames. The bumper sticker on the now-blackening rear fender read "Sigma Chi."

Then I saw the discarded, rotting, and now-half-broken skull. The false head didn't fool the murderous bastard who had killed and torched the frat boys.

Well, well.

Some machine gun-toting, car-torching headhunter was lurking out here in the sand and sage and saguaro—a real stone-cold killer—steadfastly looking for Pancho's real lid. Probably, just like me, he also had eyes on Senator Prescott Bush's eighty grand.

This was all a lark up to now—like one of my straight-to-paperback, written-for-walking-around-money "capers."

But now, maybe, our lives depended on seeing this mess through.

I slapped Bud on the back. "Let's roll, *hombre*. We've got us some graves to rob."

06

IT was starting to drizzle, so we leaned into the shovels—get that wicked work done before the rain turned the graveyard to soup. Not that it was particularly hard work. These poor Mexicans were buried as cheaply as they could be; blankets for boxes and planted so shallow I was shocked the coyotes hadn't dug 'em up long before us. We got lucky and found one skull with a pretty impressive underbite. We'd save that one for a special occasion.

Lightning slashed across the sky, illuminating young Bud and me against the rickety crosses. Christ, I felt like Colin Clive in Franken-fucking-stein.

I tossed aside my machete and pressed the heels of my hands to the small of my back. Too many bones cracked—some kind of new, dubious record. "Four heads," I said, stretching and wincing. "That should do it, Bud." We wrapped the heads up in old Indian blankets and set them in the trunk of my Chevy.

Bud presumed to take the wheel seat. I pressed the button and the canopy rose over us. I clipped down the top and we opened up

the windows, angling the wings. Big, chunky drops of rain peppered my Chevy with leopard-like dust spots.

Bud glanced over at me. "You seeing better?"

"Yeah. Better."

"Definitely blood sugar," he said.

"I should have it checked."

He nodded. "You should." I knew if I didn't see a doctor soon, Bud
would ensure that I did. He asked, "Where to now, *kemo sabe*?"

"El Paso, Tonto," I said. I rooted around my pocket and
fished out the halves of Wade's notebook. "Something called the
'Wednesday Group' that I want to look into."

We were tooling south on 54, fringing Fort Bliss. Bud saw the
signs and said, "Tell me about the Pershing Expedition, chasing
Villa. We haven't covered any of that. I'm still on *True's* nickel."

"Hard to take notes when you're driving, Bud."

"I've got a good memory. I'll get the gist of it down in El
Paso."

I shrugged and resigned myself to another trip down shitty, old
memory lane. "Not much on that front to confide, Bud. It was all a
kind of a great waste of time. National pride was at stake—the first
and only successful strike at the mainland U.S. by a foreign power
couldn't go unanswered. But it's a hopeless notion, chasing one
man in a wasteland in a country not your own—real Don Quixote
stuff. Mostly, it was a practice run for the Great War. Do you know,
the Mexicans really made the first extensive use of trench warfare
in the revolution? Did you know that, Bud? Airplanes got their
first workout down there. Machine guns, too. And, of course, the
fuckin' Krauts were arming the Mexicans, trying to open up a front
on our southern border to keep us out of Europe. It wasn't the
show—World War I was the show. The Pershing Expedition was
just a then-unrecognized dress rehearsal."

Bud nodded and glanced over at me. "You keep in touch with any of your old crew?"

"Naw. Hell no. We're talking forty years ago. And a lot of my 'old crew' never made it out of those trenches in Europe. You know, I spent too damned much of my life with Black Jack Pershing. George S. Patton was there in Mexico, too. What a world-class asshole he was." I stretched and massaged my tingling right leg. "There was a fella, name of Lee Ellroy, who I knew pretty well back when. He ended up being Rita Hayworth's business agent. Lives out in California now, I think. Another couple of guys, Frank Weygandt and Cleon Corzilius; they're both back in Ohio, now. But that's about it. Oh, and Holmdahl. He's the guy they arrested for stealing Pancho's head in 1926."

Bud smiled. "Man, I gotta hear about him."

"Not so much I can tell there, either. He's one of those shadowy guys who shapes history and leaves no real footprints. Pure mercenary. Did a tour in the Philippine Islands. Spent some time in the rurales, before the revolution. But he's like a windsock, least ways to my mind. When Juárez fell, he jumped ship and joined Madero, the fella who pulled Villa into the revolution. So Holmdahl served with Villa and later with Obregón, when Obregón was doing better than Pancho. After the attack on Columbus, when we were all dispatched with Black Jack to hunt Villa, Emil turned up as one of our guides. He was arrested in '26 for desecrating Pancho Villa's grave. Some rich Texas friends, they say, got him sprung. But Pancho's skull was never found." I lit a Pall Mall and stared off toward the Rio Grande. "Allegedly, Holmdahl stole Pancho's head for twenty-five grand paid him by Prescott Bush, that Connecticut senator who they say belongs to that Skull and Bones Society at Yale that all those frat boys are trying to show up."

Fiske chewed his lip. He grinned. "Yeah, the senator with our damned eighty grand. Why don't we just call him up and do this deal?"

"Well Bud, because someone just fricasseed our frat friends and left the fake skull behind. Someone in the know and with a machine gun, near as I can tell. And, like I said earlier, Prescott has deep ties to the intelligence community. And beyond that, I don't know him from Adam. We'd be best to try to grasp the lay of the land before we make that critical contact, don'tcha think?"

"Makes sense, put that way." Bud's skittish eyes checked the rearview mirror. His caution couldn't hurt, but I'd been watching pretty closely. We had no tail I could spot.

Bud said, nervous-like, "On that note, I wonder how the boys of Delta Kappa Epsilon are doing?"

"Gotta be better than the Sigs," I said.

It went like that to El Paso—whistling through the graveyard conversation, slapping windshield wipers and the roar of that Turbo-Fire V-8. Just a couple of writers tearing through the desert in a car whose trunk was filled with severed human heads.

07

EL Paso: there was nothing there—damned near literally.

The Wednesday Group turned out to be some kind of social club of tony Texas Republicans. A feel-good coffee klatch or some such to bolster the spirits of the GOP House minority. Some of its members, a local historian told Bud and me, were reputed to have been among those who leaned on the Mexican government (or paid it, more likely) to release Emil Holmdahl so many years ago. But it was, on balance, a dead end.

On the other hand, we had been asking a lot of questions around town—and raising eyebrows.

Now, as we moseyed through this shithole town, we began getting looks.

Hmm.

I indulged a hunch and hit the hardware store where I bought four old carpetbags. We ambled back to my Chevy and snuck a false-Pancho head into one of the bags. I stashed the others in the trunk.

"We'll take this fella with us," I told Bud. "Just in case."

"Where we going?"

"Newspaper office. We're still in border country, so if the stuff is anywhere, it's apt to be here. Let's look up some old clippings. Refresh my memory on that grave robbing."

* * *

We found an old tear sheet from the *El Paso Herald Post* dated Feb. 8, 1926.

It was breathless stuff—the purple prose of some hack writer who'd clearly scented something he thought might be a story to build a yellow-journalism career upon.

—THE EL PASO HERALD POST—SUNDAY, FI

VILLA'S BODY IS ACCUSER IN GRIM CASE

American Soldier of Fortune Jailed Following Grave Robbery

BANDIT'S HEAD HAS VANISHED

Believe Decapitation Was Made For Sale To Some Institution

Texas—(AP)—A caretaker at a

1926: Emil Holmdahl strayed across the border for what was termed "a prospecting and hunting trip." He had a crony along for the ride—some Angelino going by the handle of Alberto Corral.

Feb. 5: Emil and Alberto made a Friday-night sortie into Parral, Chihuahua to crack open Villa's grave. Bad news for Emil and Alberto; their snooping around and the many graceless questions they had posed about Pancho Villa's grave in previous days had not gone unnoticed. A caretaker told all and ID'd the "ghoulish head snatchers."

Emil and Alberto also had it tougher than Bud and me on the grave-robbing front. They had to chip through concrete to do their "wretched work."

The AP article went on:

> No satisfactory explanation has been ascribed for the gruesome decapitation, although a note left with the body said the head was to be sent to Columbus, N.M., scene of the bandit raid in 1916 that resulted in the American Punitive Expedition.
>
> Many here, however, believe the arch killer's head was filched from the tomb for surreptitious sale to some institution. Conditions about the grave offered small aid to solution of the mystery except it must have taken a number of strong men to dislodge the weighty, concrete-covering slab. Liquor bottles and corks smelling of pungent chemicals found near the grave are unaccounted for. The body was left partly exposed to view, apparently having been moved only enough for the decapitators to do their work. Villa was buried here in 1923, following his death at the hands of some disgruntled henchmen.

Bud whistled low. "*Outré*. And some real over-the-top prose there."

I sighed and rubbed my eyes. "Like you said. You know, a part of me thought maybe old Wade was full of shit. But this …" My observation hung there, unfinished.

I felt cold steel at the back of my neck. Bud already had his hands up.

Fuck on a bicycle.

I turned, slow-like. A man in a business suit had a gun pointed at my head. He was some goddamned El Paso Republican, I suspected. He was wearing a virgin-white straw cowboy hat. And, no shit, he had what looked like a starched bandana tied around the bottom of his face, coming down to a triangle point that didn't quite cover his brace of chins. The bandana was too clean and showed iron lines. With the suit and that crisp white hat, the pearl-handled .45 in his shaking right hand … well, Christ, it was like being robbed at gunpoint by some queer tenderfoot.

Fuck this.

The "bandit" spoke, a scared quaver in his voice. "The bastard's head—where is it?"

My God—he said "bastard" like he was saying "scoundrel," or "bounder."

Jesus.

"Here," I said. I reached down, lifted the carpetbag and then flung it at him. The gun pointed skyward as he involuntarily tucked his arms to catch the bagged head. With my left hand, I grabbed his gun hand—kept that sucker pointed skyward. I tugged down his bandana with my right hand. That move seemed to startle him even more, although it really shouldn't have, 'cause I surely didn't recognize him.

I pulled back, then swung hard between his eyes, throwing everything I had. My right knee followed, driven hard into his groin. As he doubled over, I flicked off his cowboy hat, got a handful of hair, and drove his face down into my again-rising knee. He fell to the floor—already out cold and sporting a brand new face.

Bud was slack-jawed. I shrugged and picked up the carpetbag. I tossed the bag to Bud. I tucked the pearl-handled .45 in my waistband.

Me and my poet, we were swiftly building ourselves an arsenal.

"Just couldn't bear to lose another head this soon, 'specially to the likes of that one," I said to Bud. "We're going through these skulls like a drunken sailor on shore leave in a whorehouse on nickel night. I'm feelin' decidedly stingy now." I reached down and picked up the bastard's white cowboy hat. It was too small for my head. (Old man used to tell me, "Hec, you've got yourself a head like a bastard cat." My mother used to make cracks, too, but I figured she'd had first-hand experience with that big old head of mine that my pap hadn't had, so I gave her a pass.)

I planted the hat on Bud and he suddenly had half-assed character.

We strode out into the newspaper's front office.

The receptionist stared at us, open-mouthed under her wicked black beehive. Her eyes were wide behind rhinestone cat's-eye spectacles. "Fetch yourself a camera, sweetheart," I said in my foghorn drawl. "I think there's a breaking news story stretched out cold in back there for you."

08

IT was a very bad night for me.

I had awesomely bad dreams, riddled with strange imagery. Sad thing was, it was all rooted in recent history.

Ice cubes ... so many ice cubes.

Hypodermics.

My little, black-haired, black-eyed daughter, squeezing my callused thumb in her tiny hand and whispering "Daddy" as the darkness closed over her.

Her mother—dark hair, dark eyes, dark heart. "The heart of another is a dark place" ... something like that. Who the hell said it? Turgenev? Ed Murrow? Howdy fucking Doody? One of those wooden cocksuckers, anyways.

More ice cubes and a bathtub. Old needle tracks. My big, beautiful and empty hacienda—the fucker destroys me.

My girls regularly ambushing me in my dreams, a year on. Sometimes in my dreams—no, strike that, call 'em "nightmares"—I pick up my Colt, put that Peacemaker in my mouth and press it to my palate. In his cups, in Key West, Hemingway used to pantomime for me "The Blessed Shot," as he had dubbed it. Papa confided to me tips for doing it right. "Get that thing in your mouth, up against the roof, pointed toward the fontanel," he'd lecture drunkenly. "Press it to your temple or under your chin and you'll just end up disfigured, or a vegetable, or both." That was Papa—always the teacher.

But in dreams—and in life—I can't ever pull the trigger on myself. Too much contrition for that flavor of presumed peace, I reckon.

I awakened with a start, wrenched from my dark dreams by thunder. It was raining again—desert storm. The windows were cracked on Bud's side and I could smell the sage and the rain. My mouth was dry and my eyes wouldn't focus. My hands were shaking and I felt nauseous.

Bud raised his eyebrows. "You okay, Lass?"

I nodded and sat up and stretched and felt more bones crack. I was too old to be sleeping in cars. Bud, probably prompted by all the knuckle-digging in my eyes and my blinking, passed me a thermos filled with iced tea. He rifled through a bag on the seat between us, then handed me a Stuckey's Pecan Log and a ham salad sandwich wrapped in waxed paper. "This'll help," he said. It did, though it took some time.

We were rolling west along Route 10, skirting the Mexican border. I had slept right through Columbus and adjacent Pancho Villa State Park—the places where all of this bad juju got rolling so many bloody decades ago. My knuckles were starting to hurt from those shots I had taken at the Texas Republican. I checked my Timex. We should have been on the other side of the Arizona border by now, but we were just fringing the Pyramid Mountains.

"You stop for a quickie while I was sacked out, Bud?"

Fiske glanced at me and turned down his mouth. "Called in a marker," he said. "Old friend of mine is a Yale grad. I wanted some more gen on this Skull and Bones Society."

I grunted and gulped down a half-a-thermos of tea and it didn't touch my thirst. "Just a kind of über fraternity, isn't it?"

Bud lit up a Pall Mall—must have bought his own pack when he stopped for my grub. He shook his head. "Naw, it goes way deeper than that, Hector."

Marty Robbins was crooning on the radio: "A White Sport Coat (And A Pink Carnation)." I know Marty. I like him. But I prefer his cowboy ballads. I turned down the volume.

I said, "Startle me, Bud."

"This *politician*,"—Bud said "politician" like he was saying "clapped-up cunt"—"this *politician*, Prescott Bush? He supposedly personally robbed Geronimo's grave and stole the Apache's head for the Skull and Bones Society's secret archive."

"Had heard that. And he supposedly paid Holmdahl twenty-five thousand dollars to steal Pancho Villa's head," I said. "We knew that, too. Or we thought we did. It's all hearsay."

"Actually, my guy told me a guy named Frank Brophy said that he and four others put up five grand to have Emil Holmdahl steal the head," Bud said. "But Brophy said it was a Skull and Bones scheme, all the way."

I shook out one of my cigarettes and fished for my Zippo. I fired her up. "That's a big range," I said, "twenty-five grand down to five grand? Big gap there, my friend."

Bud Fiske smiled. "Huh-uh. Think about it, Hector. Prescott supposedly offered twenty-five thousand dollars for the head theft. Brophy, who belonged to the Skulls and Bones too, well, he said that he and four friends put up five grand. Well, what if it was five grand *each*? Then we're right back to your twenty-five grand. Prescott may just have handed over the collective cash."

It cohered. It felt right. I could roll with it. "Yeah, I can buy it, Bud. But they didn't get the head, near as we can tell."

"Naw," my interviewer said. "Something happened between the time Emil handed it over to his confederate and the confederate was to get it to Senator Bush. That's the mystery that remains to be solved."

"So tell me more about this Skull and Bones bunch. What's the capsule history there?"

Bud fished around the bag and pulled out a short dog. He steered with his knees and used the seat belt handle to pry off the lid. Fiske drained half that sucker at a pull. "Serious kink, Mr. Lassiter," he said, dragging a sleeve across his mouth. "They track back to 1832. They've got their own building on High Street—looks like a big-assed crypt. No fucking windows. They call it 'the Tomb.' The initiates pass around the same nicknames from class to class. Some of those names are pretty demonic sounding. Prescott's son, George, a WWII hero, was a member. His nickname was 'Poppy'— admittedly *not* so Satanic sounding. President Taft was a member … Henry Luce, too. It's rumored the S&Bs are tied to the CIA and something called the 'Trilateral Commission;' the NWO and the Illuminati.

"They are initiated by two older members, one dressed as Don Quixote, the other dressed as the Devil. They bind their members to the order and secure their secrecy by making them strip down and lay in a coffin," Bud said, pressing ahead in the face of my palpable skepticism. "The suckers then have to jack off to orgasm, describing in detail their sexual experiences while the other members stand there, looking on."

Jesus pleading, bleeding Christ on a crutch. "Well, if true, that'd breed some flavor of silence, I reckon," I said. Suddenly, I was fiercely proud to have never finished high school. I said, "They sound too much like the goddamned Freemasons."

"They're purportedly linked," Bud said. "And some think the sexual confessions have more to do with eugenics than shaming the subjects. You know—useful for tracking bloodlines."

We were finally drifting into Navajo territory now. Mesas and buttes; cholla, burro weed strangler, fanwood, cottonwood, iron-wood and smoke thorn; jackrabbits, Gila monsters, rattlesnakes and loggerhead shrikes. It was merciless, it was vast and it was un-thinkingly beautiful.

"Coming up on a crossroads. Where precisely are we headed, Hector? I mean, beyond, 'Keep heading west, Bud.' We still trying to keep this meeting of yours with Orson Welles?"

"We're still Cali-bound, Bud. Emil the head thief is still on the right side of the dirt—lives out in L.A. somewhere, according to Wade's notebook. And I've got that film stuff to attend to, which makes all of this a business expense and thus deliciously deduct-ible. I owe Orson a face-to-face 'no' on a project. See no reason we can't double up on errands … settle things with Welles and maybe look up Emil."

Destination: Venice, California.

09

EIGHT hundred goddamned miles, give or take, from El Paso to the dubiously named City of Angels.

In between: motels—not *ho*-tels, but *mo*-tels; small towns; county seats; old Victory gardens grown thick with weeds. White picket fences sandblasted gray by wind-driven red dust. Railroad depots. Greasy spoons and all-nite diners. Good coffee, bad coffee … catastrophic coffee. But we drank it all, just the same, to stay awake for the long cross-country haul.

Doughnuts; pep pills sold to truckers at cash registers; sugar and more of that coffee, good, bad or indifferent.

I'm really not what you could describe as a man given to nostalgia, but it seems more and more to me that the older things are, the better they were built. The ones who came before fashioned things to last. But in this age of laminated furniture and Naugehyde upholstery … well, it all just seems to be winding down.

Someday, I thought, staring out through the bug-splattered windshield, *the highway system will wipe all this out—smother "the Mother Road" … strangle Route 66 and the Old National Trail. It* will all look alike then, whipping by at seventy or eighty miles per hour; you won't see details, won't see the citizens.

The graveyards, the towns, the Victory gardens—hell, you'll never see those. You'll never fucking see 'em. One day, probably one day soon, they would fix it so you could drive from Seattle to the Jersey shore and never see an authentic city or civilian. I smoked my cigarette and shook my head. What will we have then? What will we be? I wondered this, gazing through the bug-splattered windshield of my Chevy as my poet/interviewer drove us through the darkening desert.

I glanced over at Bud. He was sucking down his fifth or sixth cigarette by my calculation. And he was on his third beer. I shook my head at my own terrible influence.

10

TOUCH *of Evil.*

Picture this: Venice, California standing in for wicked Mexico and the mythical border town of "Los Robles."

There used to be canals threaded through Venice, but they backfilled most of those bastards in '29 when they knew the car was here to stay. Those filled-in canals sucked away nearly all the charm Venice ever held. Oil wells and cricket pumps were now in abundance.

Welles was having a false bridge built—a phony gateway to the promised land of *El Norte.* The bridge was for Orson's own death scene—a fat, tragic bastard floating out there dead in the muddy Rio Grande. A great bad man finally called home to Hell or Valhalla ... wherever all the great bastards finally go to be safely out of the way of the herd.

The crafty *auteur* was shooting almost exclusively by night to keep the studio suits and the bean counters at bay.

Orson's directing of the picture resulted from an accident—an honest-to-God *mistake.* Chuck Heston signed on as star because he erroneously thought that Orson was to direct the picture. When he learned otherwise, Moses threw around his weight—and secured weighty Welles the gig.

OW had grabbed a hold of the job with gusto, still chafing from being fucked over *Citizen Kane*; fucked over *The Magnificent Ambersons*; *Mr. Arkadin*; fucked over *The Trial* and *Don Quixote*. You name it. He lost Rita *Lady-From-Shanghai* Hayworth to fucking Ali Khan. Christ, the luck of the Irish—all that getting fucked but never *off*.

Once he was seated as director, over-eager Orson commenced upon an aggressive script rewrite. Heston's *gringo* cop became a Mexican. Chuck dyed his thinning, sandy hair black and slathered on the skin dye. He grew a pencil-thin moustache—some greaser lip gravy that looked to have been lifted from Cesar Romero. Heston's gravitas, it was hoped, would offset his falling-short makeup.

Welles next cast busty and lusty Janet Leigh in some quasi-virginal Joan of Arc role.

Call it more gone-wrong casting.

But Jesus, Leigh's sure something to look at on screen. Her character's handle? Well, that was "Susan Vargas." And with those tight sweaters, she was a Vargas girl, okay.

And Marlene Dietrich—my favorite Kraut—Welles had her playing a svelte, cigar-smoking, Mexican madam with a mystery accent who drifts in and out of the picture in two or three key sequences.

It all struck me as *insane*.

But some others I trusted who had seen rushes swore to me that the picture cohered and sizzled at some oddball, gut-to-crotch level that bonded with truth. The visuals, always great in a Welles picture, were said to be stunning. And Welles' rush-job-doctored script? That sucker was mostly cooking, sources said. On the other hand, the original material, a noir potboiler called *Badge of Evil* by "Whit Masterson," wasn't chopped liver.

* * *

Orson looked like shit. He had truly packed on the weight, but the special effects crew had added extra blubber—rubber cheeks and chins to make him a mountain. Captain "Hank Quinlan"—that was Orson's character's name. Hank was conceived as a badly widowed, Borderland "bad cop" who got the job done and usually fingered—or more often framed—the right culprits. In the still-in-progress script, Hank was depicted as addicted to booze and candy bars—layering on more lard. He and Marlene/Tanya went back. Hank had a Jones for the madam, her and her "chili" … a Hayes Office-fostered euphemism for her pussy.

Orson was doing a salutary job of keeping everyone in a Mexican mood: the dirt-strewn streets were littered with blowing, rolling scraps of paper. Mariachi music, marimbas—couldn't escape 'em. The crew was half Mexican and drunk on Tecate beer Orson had had trucked in. Orson had always been the undisputed master of atmosphere and it all was working. Christ, I felt like I was on the back streets of TJ. I felt as if I should put the arm on that best boy yonder with his ducktails and untucked shirt draped over chinos and ask him for directions to the donkey show. It felt like there should be street peddlers not just present but prevalent— pushing contraband Spanish fly, hop and little hand-carved Don Quixote statues.

Bud was just wandering around in a daze, taking it all in. For my part, I watched Welles at work.

Orson was charging through this shoot. He was under intense pressure to bring it in on time and under budget; to try and erase his mostly undeserved reputation for cost overruns and spiraling-out-of-control production schedules.

But Mr. War-of-the-Worlds-Panic-of-1938 was not happy with three key scenes he was to film in the next couple of days. Two of those were new scenes; the other was a reshoot. All of them featured Marlene/Tanya—"Hank's" ex-lover—who doesn't recognize too-fat Hank the fateful night he first returns to her place.

Welles couldn't get the words right in the scene. It wasn't cooking between him and the Kraut. Orson had been friends with Marlene for years. But he'd never got her in bed … same as Hemingway.

But Orson had somehow learned that I had bedded the Kraut. He wagered I could bring some resonant dialogue to the table.

His proposition offended me.

But I owed him a favor. Ten years on, and he'd finally called in his marker. So I felt I owed him at least a face-to-face "no"—even if his request did cross too many lines. If Marlene ever found out what he was asking of me—what he was trying to exploit—well, Orson would likely shed some weight at Marlene's hands I'd wager, and *muy pronto.*

Some stooge guided Bud and me to Welles.

That Voice—like thunder in a cave. Orson intoned, "Hector, my old friend. You made astonishing time." I eyed Fiske—sucker was instantly star-struck.

Orson patted my cheek. "You must have driven like a bat out of hell, Hec."

I slapped my poet/interviewer/sidekick on the back. "My batman. Drives like a dream. And writes the same. He's the fella you should be hitting up for script doctoring."

Orson glowered. One didn't *rewrite* Welles. No, His Eminence would grudgingly brook *feedback.* Some of that input He maybe deigned to *entertain* … and some of that He even might *implement*. But sans credit—Christ, go ask Herman J. Mankiewicz or Graham Greene if you doubt me.

The coastal night wind kicked up some strategically scattered newspaper pages. One smacked Orson on his big rubber cheek. He said, "Let's go inside and talk, old friend." Orson had fucked up his leg somehow; he was leaning hard on a cane. Ever resourceful, he was exploiting it for the role, and it worked. And my God, did he ever look huge—like a blue whale with a seven o'clock shadow. He was stuffed into a rumpled, tan suit that a family of five could live in and never cross paths.

We moved inside. Welles doffed his boxy Stetson and lit up a cigar nearly as thick as Bud Fiske's neck. "Can you believe Bogart is dead?" He said this over his shoulder.

"No," I said, "I can't. Across the river from my place, all the Mexican women are tearing their hair over Pedro Infante." The Mexican matinee star and his famous moustache had recently gone down in an airplane—the third crash the actor had suffered in his risk-taking life.

The goddamn whorehouse set that Orson had whipped up was almost too perfect. It was the sitting room from a border bordello ripped from my horny imagination. Welles, in the Voice, rumbled, "You aren't still playing with that cock piece for Sam Ford, are you?"

Bud frowned—probably tripping on "cock." I thought that Bud maybe thought the picture for Ford was something that it was not … perhaps figured me for scripting skin flicks.

No. For six months, I'd been sweating various drafts of a film treatment of a pulp novel about cockfighting: *Rooster of Heaven.* I was doing it for the famous, one-eyed director.

I shrugged. "As a matter of fact, I am. And I'm humping against a deadline for my publisher … some introductions owed for a couple of other authors. And some other things, too."

Orson waved a dismissive and meaty hand. "Surely you could stay a couple of nights here, Hector. We'll drain pitchers of sangria and eat good Mexican food and talk frankly, and maybe you can help me out a tad. We must do right by Marlene. I know you'll agree with that. She's come out of retirement for this one, just for me. If she knows you're writing for her—helping me to write for her—well …"

That sounded suspiciously like an honest-to-God co-writing credit being hinted at. At that point, I figured Orson must be desperate.

Then some flunky flounced in without knocking first. He was holding a severed head in his hands.

I felt my legs go week; Fiske went white.

The stranger handed the head to Orson, who held it up and turned it then muttered something that sounded Shakespearean through the sudden buzz in my ears.

Then I saw—it was a mock-up of actor Akim Tamiroff's head. In the rough script I'd been sent, the poor bastard with a bad wig had gotten himself strangled. The head was a prop for his death scene, replete with bulging eyes and a lolling tongue. Damned fine workmanship. Orson thought so, too. He rumbled to the special effects man, "Perfect."

The bastard left, beaming, holding the toy head.

Recuperating, I smiled and gestured at the bar. "This stuff real, Orson?"

"You know me too well, Hector. Yes. Always the transcendent verisimilitude—the result of studious attention to a thousand small and seemingly insignificant details. Always that, yes?"

"Always. Yes." *Fuck.*

I picked up a decanter and tugged out the stopper. I sniffed. "Brandy?"

Welles smiled. "Perhaps. *Probably.* My stomach is too sour for Scotch these days."

I poured three glasses and passed 'em around. "Frankly, I'm not sure Marlene and me are talking anymore."

The Kraut and me had recently fallen out over a mutual "friend:" Hemingway. Orson knew and understood this, I figured. He, too, had had a fight with Hemingway—a real honest-to-God brawl—with Marlene, my beloved Kraut, standing as witness.

Orson chuckled in resonant baritone. "I've heard about your gaffe from Miss Dietrich. You're not showing enough concern over Papa's plane crashes, it seems."

Bud looked puzzled; Orson caught it. Ever the eager instructor, he explained, "Papa—you, know *Hemingway*, lad. Papa went down in back-to-back plane crashes in Africa in, was it '53, or '54?"

I shrugged, muttered, "Search me. Haven't talked to Hem since 1937, anyway." I caught myself rubbing my jaw.

Orson pressed on. "Papa's never really recovered from the crashes. He's in steep decline now. Marlene wants Hector to patch it up with him. They were fast friends down in the Keys. Birds—of prey—and of the same feather."

Enough of this. I took a shot of brandy and slicked back a cowlick. "You had your own falling out with Ernest," I said to Orson. "Did you two ever really patch it up?"

Scenting a scoop, Fiske pulled out a notebook and pen. He sat down next to Orson. That did it for me—this could go on a good while; I'd heard this story before. I started playing around with this old pianola in the corner. Orson looked over at me and said, "It's so old, it's new again." It sounded like he was reciting from something. Then damned if it didn't start playing, and my favorite tune, too, an old Celtic air, "Tramps & Hawkers." It was evocative source music for Welles' Hemingway tale.

Orson's Voice: "Ernest had assisted in the filming of a documentary about the Spanish Civil War, lad," he said to saucer-eyed Bud. "Propaganda against the fascists. Fund-raising stuff, really. Hemingway wrote the film's narration. I was to read the Papa-penned material. But it went on too much, I thought. Too melodramatic. It needed a trim to be more lean and masculine ... you know, in the vein of the stuff by Hemingway that we all so revere."

The legend went something like this. During a screening, Ernest had made some snide remarks about Orson's delivery. Ernest allegedly said that Orson sounded "queer," or some such. Hemingway probably had a point, there.

Welles said that it was impossible to read the words Ernest had written, that they were written for the page, not the screen. Welles probably had a point, there.

Orson continued as Bud scribbled away. "Hemingway couldn't get past my direction of the Mercury Theatre," Orson said, turning down his mouth. "He thought me some kind of avant-garde, theatre faggot. So Ernest said to me, 'You fucking effeminate boys of the theatre, what do you know about real war?'"

"So you swung on him," Fiske guessed.

"No, no dear boy. He'd have killed me. I played to him. Mincing, complimenting him on his size and strength. The situation swiftly degenerated. And oh so precipitously—chairs and, finally, *punches* were thrown. All of this struggling was silhouetted against the backdrop of scenes of warfare in Spain. A real Hieronymus Bosch moment. Marlene saw it all. It was quite marvelous really—two guys like us fighting in front of these images representing people in the act of struggling and dying. We ended up toasting each other over a bottle of whiskey."

I shook my head and poured some more brandy. "Tell Bud the rest, Orson. You two didn't leave it that well. Hemingway later ended up doing that narration. They scuttled your work ... old friend."

"Yes, well ..."

Not sure why, but I felt like needling Mr. Mercury Theatre. "I heard Hemingway's version from John Huston," I said. "Hem told John that every time you used the word 'infantry'—Hems words, not mine—that you sounded 'like a cocksucker, swallowing.'"

This could go either way, I figured—Orson coming for me with his cane, or ...?

As I too often am, I was really just trying to keep myself interested.

I grinned, waiting to see what would happen next.

Orson exploded in laughter. He slapped his fat thigh and rumbled, "Ah, by Christ, I do so love that bastard. I can't imagine him dead. I'd like to see Hem again. To drink with him. I'd so love to drink with both of you—the three of us together a last time—me and you bastards dear."

Me too, maybe. But it wasn't apt to happen in this lifetime.

Bud started pressing Welles for more details.

The crew was setting up Orson's next shot outside, so color Welles expansive—no pun intended. Welles had time on his hands and an attentive audience taking down every damned word ... it all added up to some kind of bliss for Orson, I figured.

I left Welles to his accidental interview and staggered out into the balmy Venice night, clutching the decanter of brandy.

11

I followed the scent of seawater to the ocean and found the beach.

There was something shimmering and white out there. I walked out onto Orson's truncated, faux bridge—little more than a jetty with rails, really—angling to get a better look.

The effort was worth it. It was one of the extras, a pretty Mexican girl, swimming in her white bra and panties in the moonlight.

I watched her for a while.

Absentmindedly, I shook out a Pall Mall and lit it up.

The swimmer must have seen the flare from my Zippo. She immediately sank low, feet first, arms crossing over her breasts. She glared at me with the dark-eyed echo of my dead wife's and dead daughter's black Spanish eyes, long, raven hair now plastered to dusky skin. I muttered, *"Perdón,"* and turned my back to her, ass to the rail.

A few minutes later, she was standing beside me, her blue gingham dress clinging to wet curves. "That was not very nice," she said.

"I'm perhaps not a very nice man." I smiled. "But tonight I wish that I was." I offered her the decanter of brandy and she sniffed at it and then sipped from it.

She eyed my cigarette. I shook one loose, put it in my mouth and did my one-handed Zippo trick, holding my own cigarette in my left hand. I pocketed the Zippo and took the cigarette from my mouth, gently placing it between her ruby pillow lips. She arched an eyebrow. "You are Héctor Lassiter, yes?"

It wasn't really a question. I nodded.

"I recognize you from the photographs on the backs of your books." My new friend shrugged. "And I've heard much about you from Miss Dietrich. She has been waiting for you. You'll follow me, yes?"

Forever, yes.

I followed the pretty, dark-haired girl back across the beach, back across the movie set, down an alley to a trailer. I would have followed her to Galveston if she had led the way. I said, "What are you to the Kraut? Are you an assistant, maybe? Understudy, perhaps? Or something else?" I let that last hang there. Marlene, famously, wasn't one to limit her options in bed.

The girl smiled and knocked on the trailer door and stepped aside. "It was so nice to meet you, Mr. Lassiter." I gently squeezed the Mexican girl's arm. I said, "You got a name, hon'?"

She smiled and shrugged. "It is not important."

"Not true. It is very important to me."

She smiled and slipped from my grip. "So nice of you to say so."

I watched her sway away … this unnamed beauty. Her head was tipped back to feel the breeze across her long neck. She was smoking the cigarette I'd given her. I took a last swig of brandy and tossed the empty decanter under the trailer.

The trailer door opened a crack—opened with a squeak. A dark face with chiseled cheekbones was peering at me; disarmingly dark hair and burning eyes. Marlene turned her head a bit; considered me through the cracked door.

I was taken aback by her hesitation. It had been a few years, granted. We hadn't crossed paths since Paris, during the liberation, staying in touch only by phone. It had been a few miles and a few too many drinks, maybe. But, Jesus Christ, had I truly slid that much? I said, "Christ, Kraut, don't you know me? I'm Hector Lassiter."

Marlene Dietrich smiled. She feinted a playful swing at my chin. She held her thumbs just like Papa had taught her to so she wouldn't break them on impact. Gutturally, she said, "Ah, Hec, you look like hell, sweetheart."

* * *

We sat on the steps of her trailer, passing back and forth a bottle of Spanish red wine—it was too sweltering to go inside.

I took a swig, then handed the bottle back to her. "I may look like hell, but you look stunning, Mar."

Marlene smiled and sipped the wine.

In vino veritas.

She said, "You're a mess, honey. But you've had a wicked year. I'm so sorry ... so very, very sorry ... for your ... for your loss. I know what Dolores meant to you."

Dolores ... my daughter. The Kraut was right. So many months since I've heard my daughter's name spoken aloud, but my little girl had become my world in the too-short time that she was alive. Marlene sent my baby girl stuffed animals and music boxes. I could feel my composure slipping.

I took the bottle from Marlene's dyed hand and drank deeply of the wine. I smelled something from her trailer. I checked my Timex. "Christ, Kraut, you been cooking something this late?"

"Perhaps." She smiled and stroked my cheek. "How are you doing Hec? Really?"

"Surviving. Writing. Drinking. Certainly there's been too much drinking. And not enough writing. Just trying to keep myself interested. You know me—you embrace whatever keeps you in the game."

"You sound like Papa: 'First, one must endure.'" Her mentioning Hem like that ... I knew it was a set-up for the resumption of a twenty-year refrain: *Patch it up with Hem, please.*

I remembered a line Hemingway wrote Marlene in a letter. She told me she'd adopted Hemingway's casual aside as a personal philosophy. I repeated it to her: "The trick is not to 'confuse movement for action.' That said, Hem's going to have to call me, darling. He owes me the apology, you know."

Marlene reached into her pocket. She pulled out this little, dark, thin cigar. I fired her up with my Zippo. "My God," she said, "you two are like warring brothers. And about equally star-crossed. And maybe equally doomed. You should call Papa, Hector. Fix it, please, before it's too late for both of you."

"My God, darling, when did you become a fatalist?" Welles' script rewrite made it clear: Dietrich's madam was also a fortune-teller. I Bogied my cigarette and extended my right palm. "Wanna read my fortune, Kraut?"

Marlene searched my failing blue eyes. Her eyes glistened. She blew two perfect smoke rings and smiled sadly. "I'm not sure how much future you have left, Hector. I think maybe you've already spent your future, my love."

I heard something on the other side of the trailer. I put my finger to my lips and then ducked down. I searched the darkness on the other side of her trailer. Two legs and some kind of a stick were silhouetted over there. I crouched down and rolled all the way under Marlene's trailer.

I tucked my arms around the back of the spy's knees and heard this rumbling, "Shit!"

Then this mountain fell on me.

The mountain was followed by a pen and a notepad that smacked me in the face.

It was fucking Welles, spying on us—actually taking notes. I couldn't get my big hands around his bigger neck, but I was sure trying to. Orson's nails scratched the backs of my hands, drawing blood. Marlene had her arms around me, pulling at me. "Stop it, Hector. Stop it you two!"

Welles had his hands up in surrender, smiling crookedly and laughing at me.

My fucking ribs *hurt*. It felt like the enormous bastard might have cracked a couple falling on me. I struggled up with Marlene's help, one arm wrapped around my ribs. "You cocksucker!" I kicked Orson once … and couldn't tell if I hit fat or special-effect's padding. So I kicked him again. But to no discernible effect.

"You and me," I said to Welles, "we're through." I walked away as Marlene stooped to help Orson to his feet. The Kraut and a fork-lift might get the job done.

I heard Orson's resonant grumble at my back. "That bastard. Who does Lassiter think he is? That fucking degenerate drunk and wife killer! You hear me Lassiter? Who do you think you are? I'm Orson Welles!"

He screamed this last at my back.

I heard Marlene say to Welles, "Stop it, you fool. What does it matter what you say about him? He's a man … that's all."

12

I was limping down the thirsty canals of Venice when this arm slipped through mine. The Mexican girl who favored near-naked moonlight swims smiled, then sighed as she saw the bloodied backs of my hands. "Come with me," she said. "I'll clean and bandage those for you."

I obediently let myself be led along. I muttered, "Guess you saw all that."

"I saw the fat pig spying. And what happened after, yes."

I smiled and shook my head. "Because you were spying, too. Yes?"

She smiled back … and I was a goner. She said, "Just so."

She led me to her modest room located a couple of blocks from the movie set. I asked, "You live here?"

"Just for now—while we film. I'm an extra. And assistant to Miss Dietrich." The Mexican girl smiled and arched a black eyebrow. "And that title—'assistant,' I mean—is all that I am to her," she said.

Well, well. "I'm so glad," I said. I lowered myself gingerly onto her couch, my ribs burning.

The girl returned with a bottle of Merthiolate. She used the little glass wand bound to the rubber-stopper lid to slather the red, stinging medication on the fingernail scratches furrowed across the backs of both of my mangled mitts.

"I still don't know your name, sweetheart."

She pressed the adhesive bandages in place and then helped me off with my jacket. *"Me llamo* Alicia Vicente."

I let that roll around my mouth. "Alicia. Lovely name." She unbuttoned my shirt and put out her hands to help me up. She squeezed my ribs, feeling and probing through my undershirt.

I winced a couple of times as she found the spots that hurt most. "You a nurse?"

"I've had some training," Alicia said, brushing her black hair back behind her ears. "But my grandmother thought with my looks …"

"*Abuela* was right."

Alicia smiled knowingly. "I don't think they're broken Héctor … probably only bruised. But if so, they'll hurt almost like they are broken."

"Don't suppose you know anything about diabetes?"

She narrowed her eyes. "Why?"

"My friend thinks I might have it. I thought you could maybe confirm his diagnosis. And I should probably find him. He's bony; if Welles were to fall on poor Bud, well, it would be a slaughter."

Alicia helped me back on with my shirt and jacket. "Other than some of the old *pachucos* Mr. Welles has hired to play thugs, we don't have much fighting on the set. Not 'til you arrived, anyway."

"Unfortunately, it's all too often the way when Héctor is in the room." I smiled as I caught myself pronouncing my name with my new friend's Spanish inflection.

She smiled back. "I will help you look for your friend. And try to keep you out of harm's way."

"Don't get me wrong, but why would you do that?"

"You strike me as a man who needs looking after. Your luck is running dark tonight."

"I met you."

Her shoulders rose and fell. "On balance, your luck is running dark. You need looking after."

"You and my skinny friend are gonna get along great."

13

COULDN'T really go back to the movie set—didn't want to confront Orson or Marlene again.

Bud was a Midwest boy, so I wagered he was maybe walking the beach, taking in the Pacific by moonlight. Or perhaps he'd found himself one of the Mexican working girls who were camp-following the film crew … with any luck, he wouldn't get rolled after his roll with her.

Alicia's arm was linked with mine, the creaming waves almost licking our feet. I wasn't *quite* old enough to be her grandfather. But I was within limping distance. I looked at my bandaged hand and muttered, "Christ, I feel like Robert Cantwell."

"I know the book you speak of. I just read it. Miss Dietrich has been forcing copies of Papa's books on me. She thinks maybe I could play Maria in a television production being worked on of *For Whom the Bell Tolls.*"

Alicia's thick, black hair swung almost to her ass, tapering to a point just above her tailbone. "You'd have to cut off all of your hair for that part," I said. "That would be a mortal sin."

My new friend smiled and shook her head. "She's a stupid girl—Maria in *The Bell*. In the book, you know?"

"I know. I agree."

"Papa cannot write good women," Alicia said. "Not in romance, anyway ... not in the novels. They are almost all daughters and whores. The women in some of his short stories, however, well, they are different."

I couldn't resist. "Ever read my books?" A wicked thing, a writer's vanity.

"A couple. Miss Dietrich has been giving me those, in the past few days, too. You don't write stupid girls like Maria or that countess mooning over old Colonel Cantwell. But you do write about a lot of *putas* and scheming women."

"It's pulp fiction, sweetheart. I don't do romance." I gave her a good once-over and a smile. "Though you ... for you I could give it a try. I'll rechristen you 'Paloma' and we'll call the book *Across the Rio Grande and Into the Cacti*."

She smiled and wrinkled her nose. "That is terrible." She slipped her other arm through my arm, lowering her head and watching our feet. Her black hair cascaded in a veil that covered her face from my view. "Last night, I finished *The Land of Dread and Fear*, Héctor."

My most recent book ... written in a fever dream of guilt and liquor and whoring along *La Frontera* in the weeks following my family's death. I got too cute with it: tried to "subtly" use a love affair between my border agent and an unwed Mexican mother to mask a meditation on U.S. and Mexican relations. Not sure I pulled it off. And the guard ends up alone and old and dying.

Alicia said, "The girl, the young mother in your book? Marita Sanchez? She seemed quite real to me."

I stopped, turned, brushed the glistening, black hair back from her face and kissed her forehead. God, the sweet young scent and promise of her. "If I sell the movie option of that book," I said, "I'll make it a contract stipulation that you play Marita. Deal?"

She gave this the smile it deserved—the book was far too dark. It could never be a movie. "I'll hold you to it," she said with mock gravity. She got my act … and that made me want her more.

Then the gunfire started.

There was this flare of light from the pier—sixty, maybe seventy yards away. That distance and the dark were all that saved us from being cut to ribbons by the first volley. I pivoted, getting myself between the shooter and Alicia. Then we ran.

14

THE sand kicked up around our feet as the slugs dug in at the tide line. All that moonlight on silvered water made us silhouettes—too-easy targets. Running inland though, well, that would take us closer to the shooter—and off the hard-packed wet sand that was easier to run on.

I checked that distinctive flash flare from the muzzle. It was a Thompson submachine gun. I was sure of it.

I wrapped my right arm around Alicia's shoulders. With my left, I somehow drew my Colt and fired at the machine gun's muzzle flash. The flash jittered—the shots started going wide of us. I must have actually hit the bastard. But how badly? I shot again at the flare, but it was a long way away and a guess. And my Colt's muzzle flash let the bastard get a better bead on us. A skiff lay abandoned at the tide line. I dragged Alicia with me behind it, then rolled half atop her. I switched gun hands and chanced a look over the boat's hull. *Strange* … the machine gunner was firing straight up and over his head. I almost pitied the bastard when all those slugs came raining back down.

Sudden silence—no more gunfire.

A familiar voice called, "Hector, you okay out there?"

Bud Fiske. Bless him! "Shooter's down Hector—the coast is clear."

I smiled and stood, waving. I brushed off sand and extended my right hand. Alicia took it and I pulled her up to me. I helped her brush sand from her dress ... felt muscled thighs and hips through the thin fabric. Her eyes searched mine. Reluctantly, I said, "We best get up there ... make sure my friend really has it all in hand." I slipped my arm around her waist as we slogged through sand. She wrapped her arm around my waist.

We climbed the steps up to the pier. Bud was standing there, looking like the world's most rickety Texas Ranger in his white hat. He had one wingtip pressed to our attacker's throat and Wade's .45 leveled at the bastard's right eye. "I gotta get you some lizard-skin boots to go with that hat, Bud," I said.

The Tommy gun was laying several yards away. I picked it up to add to our arsenal of liberated weaponry. As I rose with it, my ribs cracked again. I walked back and squatted down next to the shooter, Mex-style—hams on heels. The shooter had taken a slug in the shoulder. I guessed that that slug was one I had fired. There was blood pooling under him, much lower down. Probably hit in the back. That would have been Bud's shot. Back-shooting—now, that ain't cricket. Not *ever*. But then, Bud was not a professional. And he was outgunned. And hell, he saved me and Alicia—who at that point I was thinking might well be the next Mrs. Lassiter.

There was blood at the corners of the shooter's mouth—some more running from his nose. Lung shot, probably. He wouldn't linger long like this. The gunner was maybe thirty. High-country

Mexican … some Indian in there. Maybe Tarahumara in the mix. "You got a handle, boy? You speak English?"

"I'm dying."

I nodded. "Probably. Why'd you try to kill me, son? Who are you working for?"

"I need a priest."

Christ. One of those.

"Not much chance of finding a padre around here at this hour," I said. "But I'm Catholic, too, and I know the words well enough, I guess."

Well, I was a Catholic, three marriages ago. I looked at Fiske and Alicia. "Anyone got a crucifix?"

Alicia was wearing one around her neck. I handed it to the Mexican, who kissed it with his bloodied lips.

"Now," I said, "you tell me who sent you after me, and why, and we'll pray with you."

Not good—he was fading faster than I expected. I thrust my thumb into his shoulder wound, bringing him back a ways. Between screams he gasped, "Fierro. We were hired by Fierro, to help get *el Jefe's* head."

I kept digging my thumb into his wound. "Fierro? Who is Fierro?" I pressed harder.

He groaned, blood bubbling from his mouth with the garbled words: "Rodolfo … Rodolfo Fierro … *el Carnicero.*"

Spanish for "the Butcher."

"You fucking liar!" I ground my thumb in hard then and accidentally passed the bastard out. "Fuck!" Rodolfo Fierro—a dead legend. *Long dead.* He couldn't be alive…

Alicia, white-faced, was clearly upset by what I'd just done, what I'd just said. She put a hand on my shoulder and squeezed hard. "Did you hear what he said?"

"Pretty clearly I did. You know of Fierro?"

Alicia angrily shook her head. "No, not that, Héctor. He said, '*We* were hired...'"

Oh yeah, "we." And just then, the second machine gun opened up on us.

15

BUD wrapped an arm around Alicia's trim waist and rolled back around the corner of the loading dock with her—good thing for them the building was brick because the shooter tracked their path with a flurry of lead. Fragments of brick rained down on me. But my friends were safe. I crouched down behind some boxes filled with something I prayed was thick and hard. I aimed the first shooter's discarded Thompson and fired back at the other machine gun's muzzle flash. I held my thrumming machine gun with one hand. It was murder on my right wrist. With the other bandaged hand, I fished out the keys to my Chevy and lobbed them over my shoulder at Bud—all that twisting and exertion was almost too much for my Orson Welles-splintered ribs.

I hollered over the din of the roaring machine gun, "You two go get to my car, and pick me up at the end of the alley. While you do that, I'll keep this bastard busy." Then I remembered fabled Fierro, and said, "Bud, you see any old Mexicans, you shoot 'em. Don't hesitate. God'll sort 'em out on the other end. No shit—shoot first." I heard four feet beat pavement down the alley. God willing, I'd follow them soon enough.

I squeezed off a couple of bursts then set the Tommy aside. I had no target, and no infinite supply of ammo. My situation wasn't looking anything near the neighborhood of good.

Groaning, I picked up the conked-out, wounded Mexican at my side. I propped him up and then lifted him up from cover and pitched him as far and high as I could to the right. My ribs burned as I hurled him up and out.

Several slugs tore through the Mexican and shredded his head and neck. I picked up the machine gun and rolled off to the left of my cover, deep into shadows. I rolled up against a pile of old, discarded burlap sacks. I pulled the sacks over me and waited.

The other shooter approached, crouched low, his gun swiveling side-to-side—a very cautious fellow.

At six feet, I let loose on him, looking just to maim him—I sorely wanted to debrief the bastard.

But it's a tricky thing, firing for flesh wounds with a machine gun at close range. I hit him, but not squarely enough. Howling, he turned, drawing a bead on me. I had to let him have it then. I went for his upper body, but my would-be assassin lost his footing, dipping a bit. All those slugs I hurled his way decapitated him. There it was—another head, rolling there on the boardwalk, but much too fresh for our collection. I patted his torso down, trying hard to avoid all the spreading and spraying blood. No wallet and no papers to be found on this fella. Ditto on the first shooter. They were pro enough to leave all the incriminating or useful stuff elsewhere, just in case they were caught or arrested.

They were nasty as hell—and hot, too, from all the firing—but I couldn't bear to leave the twin Thompsons. I grabbed 'em up with a couple of drums left by the first shooter. Loaded down with firepower for Bud's and my arsenal, I trotted down the alley.

There were sirens in the distance now. I could hear 'em better as I put some buildings between me and the muted roar of the ocean.

Thank Christ and Bud Fiske. My beautiful blue and white Chevy was sitting there like Trigger, or Rocinante—or maybe Siete Leguas, Pancho Villa's legendary doomed mare.

Alicia opened the passenger door and slid over to make room. I tossed the Thompsons on the floor of the backseat and swung in, the pretty Mexican girl sandwiched between Bud and me. I smelled her perfume and dark hair, her sweat and fear and vibrancy. She smelled like Mexico.

I told Bud, "Cops are on the way, so drive slow and easy and like we own the place."

He did.

I checked my hands—they were shaking badly. Alicia took my left hand in hers and squeezed, careful to go easy on the Orson-inflicted cuts across the back of my hand. "You are unhurt?"

"From that particular fray? Yeah."

"And the other men?"

I shrugged and rooted around my sports jacket's pocket for my cigarettes. "*Día de los muertos* time back there, darling. I'm no Tracy Richardson, but I can hit some things with one of those choppers." I jerked my head in the direction of the machine guns in the backseat. "Papa and me used to use them on the *Pilar* to kill sharks."

Two California Highway Patrol cruisers whipped past us then, headed to the place we'd left. The cops' cruisers were the same make and model as my own—'57 Chevrolet Bel Airs—but black with white doors and roofs, blue sirens screaming.

"We'll let things cool down, then see you get back to the set," I told Alicia.

The wind through the open windows fingered her raven hair. She shrugged. "It wasn't much of a job. You have all those connections with Hollywood; I say you owe me a real film role, Héctor."

"It's a deal, sweetie," I muttered, unlit cigarette dangling from my lips as I looked for my Zippo. "I've got a picture for you in mind," I said, hand still fishing around for my lighter. "Sam Ford's the director. And we're filming in Mexico. He owes me large." *Ah, my old Zippo.* I fired her up and lit my Pall Mall. Soon as it was going, Alicia appropriated the cigarette. I got a second coffin nail going. She took that one from my lips and stuck it in Bud Fiske's mouth. Three's the charm—I got to keep the third one. But the girl took my old Zippo from me. She turned it until the dash light fell just so. She read the engraving aloud:

> *To Hector Lassiter:*
> *"One true sentence."*
> *—E.H.*
> *Key West,*
> *1932*

"What does it mean?"

I took my Zippo back. "Something from an ex-friend you've been lately reading. A kind of shared credo. I remember it. Not sure he does anymore." I felt the weight of twin gazes from Bud and Alicia.

Astute Bud went for a change-up. "This Rodolfo Fierro, or '*el Carnicero*'—what's his story?"

I looked to Alicia. I was curious to see how much she knew of her country's revolutionary history. She exhaled a thin stream of smoke and tipped her head back on the seat. It was very tight up front. I stretched my left arm along the seat's back, fingertips brushing her bare shoulder. The tactile contact *could* be interpreted as an accident. "His story," the Mexican girl said, "is supposed to be over. He is supposed to have died, something, I believe, like forty years ago." She smiled apologetically and it felt like she scooted a bit closer to me. "I don't know the details."

But I did. Legends passed along the dusty, sweltering trails during the Pershing Expedition.

Rodolfo Fierro was Pancho Villa's chief assassin. Fierro is Spanish for "iron," and Rodolfo was certainly that. He was also a full-fledged psychopath—a stone cold killer of epic proportions. He was born in El Fuerte, Sinaloa in some unknown year. He was gaunt, cold-eyed and often leering. The diseased fucker favored Stetsons—a fact that made him more the asshole in my eyes.

After a rout of the enemy at San Andrés, Villa once ended up with several hundred inconvenient prisoners. Supplies were running low and bullets were precious. It was "take no prisoners" time. But there was the vexing issue of those precious bullets. Fierro struck a bloody balance. He arrayed men in rows of three, according to height, best it could be arranged. He made some men squat and made some others stand on tiptoes. He ordered them to embrace one another, to press bellies to backs. He killed three men with a single shot … over and over…

Juárez brought another slaughter. It was a similar situation: several hundred prisoners were being held in a corral. Fierro was feeling "sporting." He had a table set out. He had an array of guns loaded and spread out on that table. Several men stood by him to reload his empties. Fierro told the prisoners any man who cleared the fence at the back of the corral before Fierro could shoot him would go free. At day's end, Fierro's hands were cramped and bloody. He was seen soaking them in a horse trough. No Mexicans had cleared the fence that day. There were high piles of bodies with holes in their backs, left swelling and rotting in the Juárez sun.

At the battle of Tierra Blanca, 1913, Fierro, on horseback, allegedly overtook a Federalist train. He hopped on board and single-handedly killed the entire crew. A railroad man from way back, Fierro stopped the train—and earned a heady field promotion from Pancho Villa.

But even *el Carnicero's* luck couldn't hold. His alleged end was almost too poetic to be accepted as true.

Autumn, 1915: One of Pancho Villa's lieutenants, Tomás Urbina, something like a bastard brother to Pancho, stole a cache of Villa's gold and silver—the treasure whose location was allegedly recorded on a map hidden in Pancho's severed head.

Villa and company rode out to confront Urbina and company. Villa got sentimental and weepy—for a time. Suddenly, always-mercurial Villa turned on a dime. Pancho said, "Shoot him." Fierro was always eager to comply with a directive like that. Fierro dragged the execution out though—maiming Urbina with surgically administered shots. Then Fierro and his crew loaded their horses with bars of recovered gold and silver and rode off in pursuit of Villa.

Accounts differ regarding what happened next. One story has it that Fierro, horse heavy with bullion, drowned attempting to cross a rain-swollen stream outside Nuevo Casa Grandes. Others said he went down in a quicksand bog, screaming for help as his own men watched him sink down to hell, leaving only a hat floating on a bog.

Either way, in mid-October of 1915, Rodolfo Fierro disappeared from history.

Bud shook his head. "Jesus Christ. If the old bastard is alive, he'd be, what, around eighty?"

"Probably thereabouts," I agreed.

The young poet nodded. "And Fierro's chasing Pancho's stolen head?"

"Why not? Everybody else seems to be."

"So what's next?"

I shook loose another Pall Mall. My luck truly seemed to be improving—I got to hold on to this one, too. "We head up to L.A.—Van Nuys," I said. "I think it's time to have a colloquy with Mr. Emil Holmdahl, the mercenary and head thief." I squeezed Alicia close. "What about it, darling? Up for a road trip?" I leaned around to get a better look at Fiske. I said, "How's about you, Bud … you balk at a three-way split?"

Fiske smiled. It seemed it was all hypothetical to him. "What the hell, Hector? Sure. But it's tough to divide an even number by an odd one."

"We'll even it out from my end," I promised.

Alicia shook her head. "These crazy men after you seem prepared to do anything. I think the only way I might be safe for now is staying with you two." She narrowed her eyes and said, "But what is this of heads … of *stolen* heads?"

I smiled. "We'll get back to that. Right now, we've got another, more pressing concern." I spotted a truck stop. There were perhaps four dozen tractor-trailers, idling in the night with their running lights on. "Pull in there," I told Bud.

I rolled out, wincing as my ribs cracked again. Bud sidled up beside me. "What's wrong?"

"That slaughter back in Venice," I said, "it got me to thinking. How did those sons of bitches find us?"

Bud nodded, going white. "Yeah … how *did* they do that?"

Moaning, I slipped off my sports jacket and handed it to Bud. I popped the hood, checked the trunk … *nada* and *nada*.

I was feeling around the left rear wheel well when I felt this strange bump. I tugged hard at it and loosened this … *device.* I pulled hard against the magnet wedding it to the chassis. Bud whistled low as I held it up to the parking lot light—a black box with a chrome antenna sticking out. Bud said, "What in God's name is that thing?"

"Some tracking gizmo I'm thinkin'," I said.

"Yeah. Who put it there?"

I smiled at Bud and said, "Some asshole from El Paso, maybe. Probably working for Prescott Bush—the alleged spymaster." *Yeah.* Prescott … who clearly didn't know he was maybe employing stooges who also worked for Fierro. Or maybe Bush had actually unwittingly employed the Butcher. Which shows you what that fella, as a spymaster, apparently knew.

I looked around but saw no obvious spies. I slapped the tracking gizmo on the bottom of a tractor-trailer with Idaho plates. Let the cocksuckers chase that bad boy. Bud grinned and said, "I hope they like Boise."

I slapped his back, smiled. "They do," I said, "and they'll be the first."

16

WE made Los Angeles at dawn. My blood sugar was off again, and my vision was fading fast. Alicia had fallen asleep long ago, her head curled into the hollow of my neck. "Let's get some breakfast," I said to Bud. "We need to be sharper for this old bastard Emil. We really need to be on our game."

I treated them to the Aero Squadron—a kitschy restaurant tricked up to look like a bombed out European palace, packed with military memorabilia. It had been a few years, but it was frozen in time. It was a pricey breakfast, but God, was it ever worth it.

As Alicia and Bud finished up, I scooted to a pay phone. I dialed up Jack Webb. Laconic cocksucker owed me at least one favor. And the LAPD owed Webb many more favors.

Someone had left their *L.A. Times* in the booth. As I waited to leave a message, I flipped the paper over and scanned it. There was a banner headline about the Brooklyn Dodgers maybe moving to L.A. According to "staff writer" Cooter Wrye, in New York, there was talk of lynching Walter O'Malley. Plans were afoot to place the stadium in Chávez Ravine. *Holy Jesus.* So much for America's favorite pastime. When the ball clubs are for sale to the highest bidder and can be moved around like house trailers, what's left of the game to love? Bastards had even found a way to fuck up baseball for me.

I left my message for Webb and headed back to the table.

One hour and several Bloody Marys later, I was summoned back to the phone. Jack spilled. Well, he *laconically* spilled—telegraphically giving up the goods.

Seemed that Emil's wife, Elizabeth, had died a few months ago. Holmdahl was currently living with his stepdaughter. Mr. Dragnet shot me the address. "Now *you* owe *me* one, cocksucker," he said.

"You ever get down South, you can collect." There was an implied "asshole" on my part there at the end.

"We got a line on Emil," I said, rejoining Fiske and Alicia. She'd freshened up, brushed the wind tangles from her black hair. That lipstick she sported … Scarlet Seduction, maybe? Should be called that. I swung into the booth close to her; felt her hip pressed tight against mine.

Bud watched me scoping Alicia. Lad probably felt like a third wheel. I made a note to myself: *I gotta buy this kid a woman.*

Bud said, "Holmdahl must be as old as dirt, too."

Too?

I let that one pass. Maybe Bud was thinking of Rodolfo, the Butcher. "Yeah," I said, scowling in spite of myself. "He'd be seventy-five or upwards. But he remains in the game. He's tied up with some real estate deal in Punta Banda now, down San Diego way."

"We'll call ahead?" Bud said.

I waved a dismissive hand. "Why warn? Let's ambush the old campaigner," I said.

I checked Bud's dusty, beat wingtips. "But I want to hit a Western outfitter first. Get you a proper pair of boots to go with that hat. Holmdahl's a horseman. Let's play to his sentiment for days gone. I'll do the talking, you'll just be like Tonto—if Tonto was a cowpuncher."

Alicia had spent a couple of hours the night before, captive to a bunch of Holmdahl stories. She said, "'Sentiment?' It doesn't sound like this Mr. Holmdahl has much of a heart, Héctor."

"Naw, he really doesn't," I agreed. "But now he's getting up there and he may have old regrets that make him weak in some important places. And he lost his wife recently. Maybe that weakened him a bit, too."

She searched my eyes. Her hand brushed my cheek and she shook her head. "So we go now?" She smiled—a bittersweet, Scarlet-Seduction smile. I suddenly had the feeling she and Fiske had been talking about me in my absence … maybe talking about presumed regrets and recent losses of my own.

"Huh-uh," I said. "Not now. Now we go to bed. We're all beat-to-the-wide and look road-ragged. We'll stop and get you a couple of new outfits when we get Bud his boots. Then we'll find a good hotel. Grab some sleep and showers—bath for you, honey, if you prefer. We'll see Emil *mañana*, maybe. We need to be at our sharpest for that negotiation. This old bastard Emil doesn't draw a breath without thinking three moves out."

The unspoken, additional motive—I wanted to watch our tail for a time … make sure we were not being shadowed by frat boys; Texas Republicans; by machine-gun toting *banditos* or old Mexican ghosts nicknamed "the Butcher."

17

THE desk clerk was missing an arm. I asked, "Korea?"

The maimed clerk shook his head. "Naw. Parachuting into Corregidor, February of '45."

"You're older than you look," I said.

"That's 'cause I can't drink with both fists anymore. They shot it off before I hit the ground," he said.

I thanked him for his war service. There was some awkwardness after that.

Two rooms?

Three?

We ended up with two. Me and Fiske ostensibly in one room, Alicia in the other … a connecting door between them.

But Fiske, bless him, said he wanted to get some notes organized, then he essentially commandeered one of the rooms, leaving Alicia and me together in the other. I had to smile at Bud's excuse that he needed time with his notes for his article—as if he could truly print anything about what had been happening to us these past forty-eight or so hours.

It was real publish-and-perish stuff—write it down and you'd likely face indictment and the chair. Hell, we'd maybe face a firing squad if they extradited us to Mexico for killing those *federales*. But good ole Ike would never let *that* happen. The U.S. doesn't deport its own gringos to mere Mexico, regardless of what bad things they might have done down there.

As Alicia drew her bath, Bud and I talked, sharing a couple more cigarettes and some decaffeinated coffee. The sound of her bathwater being drawn was like a siren's song ... so hard to resist. But I hung in there.

Bud slipped off his jacket. He rolled up his sleeves a couple of turns. Unfastening his watch, he accidentally dropped it on the carpet. As he reached to retrieve it, his sleeve rode up. It was like a shot to the kidney.

Christ, Are those fucking needle scars there just below the crook of his elbow?

My stomach knotted tighter. *Easy, could be a trick of diabetes-afflicted vision*, I told myself. But I filed it away. I'd be watching. Particularly since this kid had my back. I sure as hell didn't need some junkie Tonto. And I really didn't need some inverted Sherlock Holmes and Watson relationship with the great detective's sidekick doing all the shooting up.

"Hard to know when we'll get another chance to get some sleep, kiddo," I said, trying to sound friendly—just like always. "So you try and get some rest, Bud."

Fiske shook his head. "You should talk."

I backed out, smiling and closing the connecting door between us.

The bathroom door opened. Steam rolled out through the widening crack. Alicia was wearing one of my shirts, the sleeves rolled up several turns at each arm. And those rolled-up sleeves instantly reminded me of my worries regarding Fiske. *Fuck!*

She pulled a comb through her damp, black hair, making tracks, and sat on the foot of the bed, tucking one dusky leg up under the other. I saw a flash of white cotton panties, and, just like that, Bud Fiske was forgotten.

Alicia smiled uncertainly. "Everything is alright, Héctor?"

"Getting there." I rubbed my chin; two days without shaving. I could feel—hell, I could *smell*—the dust and sweat on my skin and hair. And, of course, I was saturated in the stench of all of that cordite and nicotine. "Gonna grab me a shower." I smiled, shrugging and unbuttoning my shirt. "You don't have to wait up."

Alicia flashed a knowing smile. "No, I don't."

* * *

I finished shaving and sourly appraised myself in the mirror.

Regardéz: Hector Lassiter at fifty-seven.

The liquor was maybe a week away from putting some worrisome and irreversible weight on me. The capillaries in my nose and cheeks looked like they were ready to go. My once dark brown hair had faded to brindle and was now well on its way to gray.

I wasn't the man I remembered being … or at least not the guy I remembered thinking I was. No longer the man who could clear a bar or win the heart of any woman for at least the long week it would take her to tumble to the kind of man I really am.

No longer the man who could endlessly write words that burned.

I hitched a towel around my waist and padded out, massaging my aching ribs.

I sat down on the bed. Alicia had the sheet up over her breasts. I stroked her bare shoulder. "You sure about this?" I asked. "I'm old enough—"

Alicia pressed her hand to my mouth and said, "You're old enough to know what to do."

She turned the radio on, presumably to set the mood and maybe spare Bud the sounds through the walls.

Johnny Cash for the nervous talk, "Give My Love To Rose."

Foreplay: Mathis crooning "Chances Are;" Sam Cooke and "You Send Me." Tender, slow kisses and caressing hands. Holding close, moving slow and hard together, her arms tight around me; her legs wrapped around me too, making me forget, at least for that long, how much my ribs hurt.

Afterward, hearts pounding at one another: Patsy Cline, "Walkin' After Midnight;" Peggy Lee and "Don't Smoke in Bed."

All my scars—my new, Mexican darling raised her black eyebrows, her fingertips tracing the welts, the knife-blade furrows, the bullet holes and the ancient cigarette burns. She lingered longest on the crisscrossed whip scars covering my back and wondered aloud, "How in God's name?"

"You really don't wanna know."

Based on past experience, I'd made some observations of my own. She'd had at least one child. I risked sharing my theory on that.

"Her name is Azucena," Alicia confirmed with a sad smile. "Well, that's her real and private name, anyway. She's got my coloring, but blue eyes and sandy hair. I'm hoping she'll pass ... so her name to the world is Jessica. She's living with my mother while I try to make us some more money."

"How long since you saw her last?"

"Almost a month."

God. "How old is she?"

"Three."

My stomach kicked. "Three is an important age. They start to get really interesting then. Start becoming the person they will be. You should try to work things out so you can be with her now ... shape her."

Alicia smiled sadly. "The money ..."

"What about her father? What happened there?"

"Not sure. I was attacked outside the restaurant in L.A. where I was working, on Hope Street. There were three of them. They dragged me into an alley and ..."

Now I was on fire. "They were never caught?"

"No. Me being Mexican, I'm not sure how hard the police looked, you know?"

I knew. My big fingers combed through her glistening, black hair. I asked her some questions about her child, about where she lived in Los Angeles ... eventually drew out her mother's name and general location. I committed them to memory. It was just enough for me to track her down proper later, when this bandit's head stuff was wrapped up. I'd know soon enough where to start sending the money.

And, Christ, but my house back in New Mexico felt so empty. Maybe I could just move 'em all in ... Alicia and her baby girl ... and *abuela*. Fill that old hacienda with life again. Get a dog. Yeah ... so comforting to dream. Hemingway ambushed me suddenly: "Isn't it pretty to think so?"

"Pretty to think what?" Her brow wrinkled.

Holy Christ, I was monologing out loud—must really be getting senile. I shook my head, tracing the line of her jaw with my scarred and bruised hand. "Pretty to think how it would be if I was twenty years younger ... the life we might have had together."

Her fingers traced the lines around my mouth. "Those dimples of yours. When you smile, you look twenty years younger, Héctor. You should just smile more often."

"I need a reason."

"Haven't I given you one?" She nestled in, her breasts pressed to my chest, her arm enveloping my aching ribs, her thigh drawn up over my thighs. We fell into a deep sleep to the sound of rain.

18

WE awakened to an explosion.

There was a sharp report outside … could have been a gunshot, or maybe just a car backfiring. It was unexpected, so I couldn't be sure, either way.

I slipped from the bed and stepped into my pants. I scooped up my Colt and edged to the window. There was the glare of morning sunlight through the L.A. smog, but nothing particularly sinister in sight out there. I edged over to the connecting door, tapped once and then opened it.

Bud Fiske was sitting on the foot of the bed, naked to the waist. His hair was wet and slicked back from the shower. He was just replacing the hypodermic in its case. His left arm and his belly were riddled with scars. I tossed aside my gun and dove for him, trying to get my hands around his scrawny neck. Two words snarled from my twisting mouth: "Fucking junkie!"

Fiske screamed, "No!" and got his hands up and blocked my hands from getting to his throat. He kneed me in the crotch and we both tumbled off the side of the bed. I hit the floor first, right on my rickety ribs. The impact robbed me of my wind. Fiske slid his leg over me and got his hands around my wrists, trying to pin me down. It worked for about a minute. But I had two inches and a hundred pounds, easy, on Bud Fiske. I upended him, scrambled atop him and finally got a grip on his throat. The skinny bastard squeaked out, "I'm di—"

I squeezed harder and cut off his air, snarling, "That's right you fucking traitor junkie, you are gonna die."

I felt this sharp crack behind my ear and saw lights.

I reached to the back of my throbbing head, tumbling off Bud Fiske. As I rolled onto my back I saw Alicia, wrapped in a sheet. The copper ice bucket she'd taken from the bathroom sink and hit me with fell to the carpet.

She said, "Are you alright?"

She asked that as she ran to Bud Fiske.

Fiske struggled up onto one elbow, rubbing his neck with his other hand. I struggled up too.

The young poet, my trellis-thin Boswell, took one look at me, cocked and let fly. His right caught me just under the left eye. I saw stars again. Fiske grabbed a handful of my graying hair. He was all lion now. He snarled into my face, "I'm a fucking diabetic, Hector! I tried to tell you, you cocksucker. I'm a fucking diabetic!" He let go of my hair and my head bounced on the tile floor. I saw more stars.

Alicia helped Fiske to his feet.

He picked up his hypodermic vial. "Insulin, Hector," he said. "It's insulin, not fucking heroin. Jesus Christ, Hector."

I struggled up onto my elbows. "Alicia, sweetheart, leave us alone a minute," I said, rubbing my eye. "Please? Just give me a minute with Bud?" Her eyes were still blazing at me—like she really hated me.

She glanced at Fiske and asked, "Do you want to be alone with him, Bud?"

"*Sí. Gracias*, Alicia."

She smiled uncertainly. "*De nada.*" She bent over, holding the sheet over her swaying breasts with her left arm. With her right hand, she picked up the copper bucket she'd brained me with and tossed it to Fiske. "Just in case, yes?"

He smiled and pitched the pail onto the bed. "I can handle myself."

Alicia backed out and closed the connecting door behind her. Fiske shrugged into his shirt and buttoned up past the needle scars on his belly. He extended a hand and I took it. He wrapped his other arm around me and helped me to my feet. My ribs hurt … my eye hurt … my cheek hurt … my head hurt. And I felt sick inside. "Kid," I groaned, "I'm so fucking sorry."

"Yeah," Fiske said. "Sure. Now you know why I'm so attuned to your own sugar problems—first-hand experience."

"I get it now."

"What if it had been the other way? What would it be to you?" Bud shook his head. "Christ, Hector, I've seen you put away a bottle of whiskey a day—sometimes along with a couple of beers or a bottle of wine. You smoke two packs a day, easy. You've got more than your share of monkeys clinging to that scarred back of yours. So what's it to you if I was shooting smack?"

I limped to the side table and liberated a couple of Bud's cigarettes. I picked up the hotel's complimentary book of safety matches and struck one and fired us both up. I set an ashtray between us on the chenille bedspread and shook the match out and dropped it in.

"We off the record, Bud?"

"Sure."

"I mean it, friend." I don't expect he felt much like a friend about then, but I plunged on as though he was. From my direction he was. Maybe even more than a friend, now. "Nobody gets this story but you," I said. "And you never share it, right? Swear?"

"On my life, Hector. But the talk about what happened between you and your wife has been out there for a while ... you know that."

"But not the reasons. And I've never confirmed the other—my wife's addiction—not to anyone, Bud. My wife, Maria, *was* a heroin addict. For *years*. She hid it well from me. She shot up between her toes. Through the soles of her feet. Under her arms so the scars could be confused for razor stubble. Shot up through her pubic hair when she could will herself to do it."

No words needed there. Bud just nodded, sucked down some smoke.

"That was bad enough. But my daughter, Dolores, she was born with a hole in her heart ... and other birth defects. From day one, it was just one thing after another for my little girl. Eventually, the latest in a long line of doctors told me he thought my daughter's problems might be a result of her mother's addiction. Meant to warn me off having other kids with Maria, I guess. Almost on first meeting with my wife, that particular sawbones correctly deduced what I had never suspected ... even though I lived with the woman, and slept with her. The doc *knew* when he looked at Maria. I didn't know until he told me. He broke the news just a few hours before my little girl died of the birth defects caused by my wife's addiction. I confronted Maria later, after we lost Dolores, and she confessed it all. Then Maria tried to turn me into a junkie."

Bud sat there, perched on the end of the bed, waiting to see if I'd go the distance ... maybe confess complicity in my wife's infamous overdose.

But I'd gone as far as I was prepared to. "So," I said, blowing smoke through both nostrils, "that's why I attacked you when I saw the needle and all those scars. When I got a glimpse of the scars on your arm last night when you reached for your watch. It ate at me. Then walking in here this morning and seeing all your scars ... seeing that damned needle and hypo ... well, you know ... took me back to bad places. I made a shitty deduction and acted on it."

"I understand how it could happen." I hadn't gone far enough for him.

"I'm so fucking sorry, kid." I went ahead and said what I thought he must be thinking. "I might have killed you if Alicia hadn't brained me with that damned bucket ..."

"You might have," Bud said. He reached into his pocket and pulled something out. I heard a click and a swish. He held the switchblade up to catch the morning light through the window. "Or I might have killed you, Hector. I was in the process of deciding when she hit you."

I took a deep breath and rubbed my eye.

Alright then.

I said, "Good. That's good, Bud. There won't be a next time, but if there ever is ... don't hesitate."

Bud smiled. "I ain't saying 'likewise.'"

I laughed and stood up, cracking all over. I extended my hand. "We're okay then?"

Bud took my hand and shook it. "We drive on." He nodded at the wall between our rooms. "What do you tell her, though?"

"I don't know yet."

Bud slipped on his socks, tugged on his new boots and snagged his room key. He put on his hat and clipped some shades over his glasses. "Use my shower. Clean up. I'll take her to breakfast ... patch things up for you."

I searched his eyes behind the sunglasses. "You sure about that?"

"Leave it to me, Hector."

Would Bud tell Alicia what I'd just confided to him? Probably, if he thought it was necessary to mend things. But maybe he'd be so smooth it wouldn't be needed. Hell, he *was* a fucking poet, after all. And I was past caring, either way. "I'll owe you three times, then," I said.

Bud Fiske said, "How do you figure?"

"You've saved me three times. Once in Mexico, putting that pic in the *federale's* eye; a few minutes ago, when you had every right to shiv me and chose not to; and making things okay with Alicia again."

"Haven't done the last yet." He smiled and shook his head, his hand on the doorknob. "Hector, do you deliberately make a mess of your life just to keep yourself interested?"

I chuckled and shook my head. "Kid," I said, "you're the first person in this screwed up excuse for a world to really get my act. Well, the first who isn't a woman to get it."

Bud Fiske smiled sadly. "My God," he said, "what a terrible way to live." He hesitated, then said, "You know, there's a big difference between living for the moment and really trying to live in the moment, all the fucking time, Hector. The first is just wrong-headed and shallow. The latter is not only impossible, it's downright dangerous."

I remembered something Hemingway said to me in Captain Tony's so many years ago. I said it aloud: "We all have a right to hurt ourselves."

"No," Bud said. "It's plenty dangerous to you living like that, but it's also dangerous to the poor bastards closest to you. It's not right for you to choose for them."

I shrugged. "Maybe not. But you know, Bud, poets have to try to live in every moment ... and then live to write about it. It's the path you've chosen for yourself. You may not know it yet, but that's the truth. Got to feed the beast; feed the hungry muse so she'll spread her legs for you."

He nodded, but looked skeptical.

19

AFTER Bud left I sat there, staring at my hands. They were blurring out on me again.

Alright. I was officially starting to worry myself, now.

If Alicia was still talking to me when Fiske was done working her over for me, I'd ask her to find me a good doctor to help with my diabetes. And I needed an eye doctor, too.

In the meantime, I needed some grub to stabilize my blood sugar, but I couldn't hardly hit the same restaurant as Alicia and Bud. I finished dressing and checked my face where Bud cuffed me. Skinny sucker threw a creditable punch—the bruise was already asserting itself.

I locked up and walked a block to a diner that promised "breakfast all day." The eternal and omnipresent beehive-capped waitress popped her stale chewing gum and called me "hon" by way of greeting.

Two other customers were perched on stools at the counter. They were an improbable pair. The first was an ugly fella with bad skin and an enormous red nose. He was drinking coffee with a midget decked out in cowboy boots and toddler-size Levis. The mismatched duo looked like they were trying to burn off the previous night's beer buzz with the acidic black coffee.

I ordered eggs overeasy with sides of toast, sausage and bacon and my own flask of black coffee. The coffee came first, of course. I poured myself a cup and took it along to the phone booth in the back. Inside the mahogany phone cabinet was a stool and a little writing shelf. I set down my coffee and pulled out my notepad and Mont Blanc and flipped to a blank page. Then I dialed my answering service.

Marlene Dietrich had called.

Orson Welles had called.

Sam Ford had called.

Someone described to me as "an older, very rude, Mexican-sounding gentleman who couldn't or wouldn't speak English" had called. I got a phonetically transcribed version of what he purportedly said. I wrote it down, played with it, and eventually figured out what it must have been: *"Muerte a los gringos."*

Very nice, that: "Death to the Americans." My mind, of course, immediately went to Fierro. *El Carnicero.*

Sam Ford could wait.

Orson Welles could go fuck himself if he could ever position his hands around his own girth in order to do so.

Fierro(?)—the Butcher(?)—left no number where I could reach him.

"There's one more," the honey-toned voice on the other end of the line said. "A Senator Prescott Bush called." With suddenly clammy hands, I scrawled down his number.

I hung up and stared at Bush's number for a minute or two. The spooky bastard and his reputed intelligence connections had me cowed. Christ, he could probably arrange to trace a call like nobody's business. Probably could have J. Edgar's goons growing from both of my arms before I could rack the receiver.

Well, *fuck that.* For now, least ways.

I called Marlene back—called her collect, just as she had instructed.

Straight out of the gate, she asked, "Alicia is with you, Hector?"

"Yes. And she's fine."

"All these shot-up bodies …"

"Trouble found us. Well, found me and a friend. Alicia got swept up in it. No fault of her own, though that hardly matters. Circumstances being what they were, I couldn't really leave her behind."

"You swear to me that she is truly fine?"

"Truly. She is 'truly fine.' I swear."

"You see that she stays that way, Hector. Whatever it takes." Marlene hesitated. "She … has a little girl, you see. Her daughter is about the age of—"

"I know."

"It's just that—"

"Sure. I know, Marlene." I rarely ever used the Kraut's first name—doing so now brought her up short.

"Alright then," she said. "Of course." She tried then to put on a cordial face. I could hear her forced smile in her voice. "Orson is desperate to talk to you. He feels terrible."

"If you knew the back story, Kraut …"

"I do know it, love. He told me, after you fought. Orson needs this film, Hector. I'm willing to let him draw on what we two shared if it will help him make a perfect film. If I'm willing to do so, what earthly objection can you have?" That sounded more like an ac-

cusation than a question. "Do you know that you cracked one of
Orson's ribs?"

I shrugged. "Big so what? He got at least six of mine," I said.

"Hector …"

"Aw, Kraut … I abhor this. But you know, if I were similarly
inclined—agreeable, as you say that you are—I have this other
bloody business to contend with, and I know Orson is pressed for
time. Not sure our schedules can be made to blend."

"What exactly *is* going on? What is this other 'bloody
business'?"

"I'm not completely sure I really have a handle on it yet," I said.
"It's just something that has happened and—"

"Bullshit! That's beneath you, Hector. Alicia is in danger because of this, isn't she?"

"Yes. She was in the wrong place at the wrong time. Just like I
said. Nobody could see it coming. With me, or away from me, she's
a potential pawn until this is played out. At least if she's with me, I
can try to protect her. I'll lay down my life to shield her," I said.

That last sounded too melodramatic to my own ears.

Marlene snorted softly. "A pledge like that might mean something if you actually valued your own life." She sighed. "She loves
your writing, you know? More even than Papa's writing. When his
old dog has to be shot by your revolutionist, Perdido, in *Wandering
Eye*—you know the scene of which I speak? Well, Alicia sobbed
over those wonderful words of yours. We talked about your writing for hours these past few days. She has an old and steady soul,
Hector. A soul sounder than yours, if I might dare say so."

"You just did, Kraut."

"That was harsh of me. I'm sorry for that."

"Doesn't mean you weren't right."

"Alicia wants a life close by her little girl," Marlene said. "But money is tight. And you know, a Mexican girl like her, pretty as she is, well, she will never make that kind of money in Hollywood. Not now, nor for many, many years. If you'd grow the hell up, Hector—stop courting disaster at every fucking turn just to get your blood pumping—well, you might, in a very real way, reclaim the life you had for those four years."

"No," I said, grinding my teeth. "Let's amend that. The life I *thought* I had for those four years. Turns out that life was a fucking lie."

"Not all of it. Dolores was real enough."

"All too real, darling," I agreed. "But not any longer. And now you're pushing too far—even for you."

"It's too early for you to die, Hector. You have words to write. Scores to settle. Fences to mend. Friends to reclaim. And maybe another dark-haired, dark-eyed little girl to raise to womanhood."

"Kraut ... *darling* ..."

"Write this down," she ordered. "Do it for me."

She recited a series of digits and I dutifully recorded them. "What is this, Kraut?"

"A phone number. Just keep it with you. I won't ask you to use it now. Just promise me that you will carry it with you for a while. For a good while. Do it for me. Won't you do that, Hector?"

"What kind of number is this? Where in hell does this number ring?"

"Cuba," she said.

Of course. "Finca Vigia, yeah?"

"Just carry it with you a time. Maybe one night, you'll feel like using it."

I cradled the receiver between cheek and shoulder and tore the sheet of paper with Ernest Hemingway's number from my notepad. I was about to crumple and discard it when Marlene lashed out at me. "I heard that—the paper tearing! Promise me you will keep it, Hector. Fold it up and stick it in your wallet and forget it is there if you will, but promise you'll carry it. It … it means luck to me. You know what 'luck' means to me, Hector. I know that you know that."

Goddamned superstitious German chanteuse.

Marlene famously met Hemingway on a transatlantic passage. She had been invited to dine with a large party and realized she would be the thirteenth at the table. Hemingway overheard. Papa's the superstitious sort himself … always carrying little coins and pebbles and rabbits' feet for good luck. Hemingway offered to join Marlene to make it fourteen. And they were off to the races.

I folded up the sheet of paper and shoved it into a slot in my tri-fold wallet. "I just stashed it. For you, Kraut."

"*Gracias*, Hector. You two must settle this. For me, yes, but for yourselves."

I shook my head. "I don't lightly give up an old friend like that, you know. Hem and me go all the way back to Italy, and our teens. We were both shot up working for the Red Cross. Shared Paris in our twenties. That first festival at Pamplona. He and me came up together, Marlene … two of us share so many memories and losses. There's scads of stuff that I can only truly talk about and reminisce about with him. Losing Papa as a friend is like cutting off a part of myself—denying myself vast chunks of my own history and experience. So I don't do this lightly, you see—I'm not pissed on some whim."

"I hear you. Someday, perhaps, you will tell me, or he will, what happened between you two."

"Perhaps."

"Well, for now, you work this other business out, Hector, and do it fast," Marlene said. "Keep Alicia safe. Then get back down here. Orson feels terrible for what happened."

Fucking Welles—he called me a wife-killer, and his being right didn't make it go down any easier to me. But I just said to Marlene, "I'm working on it."

"Stay well, Hector."

"You too, Kraut."

I needed to shake that conversation, so I went ahead and called up Sam Ford, my dissolute, one-eyed, director buddy. He was in some place called Glasscock, Texas and drunk out of his mind. Sam wanted me to "roll east to where I am." Where he "was" was some cabin along Mustang Draw, not so far from Odessa—holed up with an Underwood and a crate of whiskey and three Mexican whores. I told him I was tied up in L.A., but would try to get back to him soon.

I looked at Prescott Bush's phone number again. I picked up the receiver and dialed the operator—then hung up before anyone answered. I needed to think it out more before I made that contact.

My breakfast had arrived. I headed back toward my table. The big drunk and his midget friend had cleared out for parts unknown. Just a trio of college-age boys sat at the counter now, drinking orange juice and stirring around scrambled eggs.

I poured some more coffee and smoked another cigarette and thought about Pancho Villa's head. I hadn't given it a good look since all this began. I hadn't checked that rotting scalp for traces of some tattooed treasure map. I hadn't probed the nose holes and eye sockets for scrolled-up scraps of paper or other clues; hadn't searched for some scrimshaw map carved into bone, maybe.

I hadn't shaken that sucker to see if anything rattled inside Pancho's rotten head.

It was high time that I did all that.

20

I settled up and stretched and cracked my back and wandered out onto the street. It was already getting muggy and the smog lay thick across downtown L.A. The storefronts of the shops across the street shimmered and wiggled through the curtain of exhaust fumes.

The first punch was to my right kidney—furious pain and I fell to my knees. A hand tangled in my hair and I took a kick to the gut. "Get him up," I heard.

It was the three kids from the diner.

Of course.

I coughed and tried to get my breath. Being lifted and forced to stand was agony on my kidney. I suspected I'd be pissing blood for the next couple of days. I choked out, "Skull and Bones?"

"That's right."

"How'd you assholes find me? Getting help from the senator and the CIA?"

"Something like that. But probably we could have just followed all the bodies you left along the way. Now where's the head?"

"Back at my motel."

"We'll walk you there, old man."

I nodded, biting my lip until it bled ... fucking kidney shot had really done me some damage. I heard tires squealing and saw the car slowing as it approached us—a ragtop Caddy with four Mexicans inside. Three were young Mexican guys; one was an old, white-haired Mexican with a big moustache and leathered face. Instinctively, I went prone—hugged the pavement.

The blast from the Tommy gun shredded through the college boys and exploded the windshields of parked cars in front of us. The storefront display windows behind us splintered and fell. As the slugs dug in past my feet, I struggled up and began half-running, half-limping in the direction the car had come—trying to put some distance between me and the Mexicans before they could swing their big Caddy around for another pass. I figured they didn't mean to kill *me*—not until they had Pancho's head, anyways. But the thought of being in the hands of a sadistic madman like Fierro? Frankly, that bloody prospect terrified me.

But that kidney shot was slowing me down. I fished around under my jacket for my Colt. Another car swerved around the corner. It was my Chevy. Alicia was driving and Bud was riding all-too-literal shotgun. They skidded to the curb and I ran around to the driver's side. "Over the seat, Sweet," I barked at Alicia. She slid over into the back and I slipped behind the wheel.

I got my Bel Air in gear and yelled to Alicia to lay down on the floorboards behind the front seat.

The Cadillac was just turning the corner.

I accelerated and steered straight for it. At the last moment, I veered to the right, palming the wheel with my right hand. I extended my left arm out straight, Colt in hand, and shot the Mexican driver in the face. The Caddy veered and slammed into the side of a newspaper delivery truck. One of the Mexicans in the backseat—the one who had fired a Thompson at me—flew over the front seat and landed on the pavement, face first and twenty feet from the Caddy.

Two down.

I was preparing to swing back around and take out the others—finish Fierro for good—when I saw the cop cruiser in the distance. Some L.A. flatfoot's routine patrol was about to go very crazy on him.

Cowed, I righted my Chevy and headed back toward our motel. "You guys come looking for me for a reason?"

Bud nodded and slipped his shotgun down out of view. "We got back to the hotel and the proprietor was out front, watering his garden. He said several people had been by asking after us—some college kids and some Mexicans. We packed up quick, and left a message with the clerk to have you take a cab to the Aero Squadron to meet up with us again. It was just an accident that we spotted you when we did."

"Happy accident."

"We deserve some luck," Bud said.

Alicia sat up behind us and brushed the hair from her face. She pulled out a scarf and tied it over her head and slipped on a pair of black Wayfarers. "You looked like you were hurt, Héctor—unable to run," she said.

"College boys from Yale got a good shot into my kidney just before they got turned into confetti. Hurts like a son of a bitch."

"Pull over," Bud said. "I'll drive now."

I pulled over. Alicia slipped back in front between us and I squeezed in. She rested her hand on my knee. Fiske—that silver-tongued devil—I did owe him thrice.

Bud said, "Which fraternity is going to be seeking new pledges?"

"Those dead boys were authentic Skull and Bones."

"No shit?"

"That was Fierro back there, wasn't it?" Alicia asked.

"Yeah—for sure it was him. The Butcher. Could see the Fierro I remember from newspaper photos and the wanted posters in that old face."

Bud smiled and shook his head. "Too strange. So what now?"

"Now we get some new digs. Hotels and motels are out of the question, now. Fuckers will scour every one of those in greater L.A. for us."

Alicia arched a dark eyebrow. "What then?"

"Pull over a second," I ordered Fiske. He did and I struggled out and limped over to the newsstand. I picked up a copy of the *L.A. Times*. I pulled out the classified section and binned the rest. I searched the ads, arms held out a distance to see the tiny type better. "Here we go. There's a little Hollywood court apartment with a garage. So let's go claim our new bungalow. Ad claims Tom Mix once slept there."

Bud Fiske said, "I loved Tony."

Alicia looked at the poet.

Bud said, "Tony. You know—Tom Mix's horse."

Alicia mouthed, "Oh …"

"It's a guy kind of thing," I said.

21

OUR new place came furnished—two bedrooms, small kitchen. Came with a radio, too—a big, old floor model Motorola with tubes and lights. Bud fiddled around with the dial on that monstrosity and coaxed loose a newscast.

The morning's shooting was being passed off as flaring Mexican gang violence; the Skull and Bones crew was presumed by police to have been confused for some rival gang. The ghosts of the Zoot Suit Wars loomed.

It strained credulity, but, hell, at least we were kept out of it. No arrests were reported, so I could only deduce that Fierro and his surviving crony had walked off from the wreck before the cops spotted them. Fierro seemed to have been granted more lives than a litter of bastard cats.

Bud and me went to the garage and retrieved Pancho's skull. I brought along the fake head, too—the best of the phony skulls with the underbite—for good measure.

Alicia said, "What are you doing with those heads?"

"Full disclosure time," I said. "You two should know some other legends about Pancho's head and some of his lost loot. Stuff about treasure maps and the like. Stories that might make us all richer." As I toyed with Pancho's skull, I filled my friends' heads with Tex-Mex treasure folklore.

I thought maybe she would closet herself while I fooled around with Pancho's head, but Alicia stayed close by the action. She brewed us up some coffee while Bud and I looked the head over. If there was ever a tattoo on the scalp, well, it was lost now. No carvings there in bone that any of us could detect, either.

Took me about six minutes, but I finally found this hairline bump trailing down out of the wispy, remaining hair, down the forehead toward the nose and then veering off and into the orbit of Pancho's right eye. The bump was just raised a bit from the surface of the skull and of slightly different hue.

Granted Pancho wasn't embalmed well, but looking at the skull now, I thought about the steps that would have to have been taken to hide something all those years ago in that much fresher head. I figured Emil and his cronies must have had pretty strong stomachs to skin down to bone whatever was left of Villa's mummified soft tissue; to maybe have to clear material out of the eye sockets and whatever was left in the head in order to accommodate whatever they might have hidden inside the skull.

I took out my Swiss Army knife and used the dull edge of my bottle-opener to scrape away at the bump. The surface of the welt flaked off like old plaster or something similar to it. There was a thin string hidden under there—something like fishing line, maybe.

I slipped the flat edge of my blade under the string and raised it, and the rest of the welt crumbled away as the pressure I was exerting on the string popped it loose. I grabbed the end of the string where it disappeared into the eye socket and coaxed loose the other end. It emerged secured to a small glassine tube, about the width of a cigarillo and maybe an inch-and-a-half long. I detached the tube from the end of the string. I said, "There's some kind of paper rolled up inside there."

Alicia loaned me her tweezers and I teased the paper loose and carefully unrolled it. It was square. Unfolded and unfurled, the scrap of paper measured maybe three inches by three inches. The paper was yellowed with age and appeared to be blank on both sides. There was a notepad of blank paper by the phone. I asked Fiske to fetch the pad. I carefully traced the outline of the hidden scrap of paper and cut out a match from the notepad. "An eventual replacement," I said to Alicia when she arched an inquiring eyebrow.

Bud leaned in and looked at the old scrap of paper. "The map?"

"Must be. Or must have been—nothing to be seen on it now."

"Invisible ink maybe?"

"Only thing it could be."

"Great," Fiske said. "So we'll need to get the information from Holmdahl about making the writing appear to have any shot at how to get at Villa's gold. It's looking like a four-way split."

"Fuck that," I said. "This thing was probably prepared on the fly, down there south of the border. They would've used whatever was at hand, and that couldn't have been too fancy. So I'm betting the ink they used would've been milk, lemon juice … maybe vinegar, or most probably, their own urine."

Alicia wrinkled her nose and muttered "Yuck."

"In any of those cases," I continued, "heat will bring the writing up. We got any candles around this joint?"

Bud found a pair in the cabinet over the range. The last inhabitant of our bungalow must have been some Klansmen or *Amos and Andy* fan who liked romancing fellow racists—the candles were attached to some wicked candleholders. The wax sticks of the candles were gripped in the exaggerated lips of these little, ceramic minstrel faces.

I lit one candle with my Zippo, sat the repugnant Step-and-Fetch holder on the table, and picked up the scrap of paper with the tweezers. I nodded at the note-pad and said to Bud, "Get a pencil and be ready to get this down. It's old and the writing may be very faint ... it may also evaporate very fast. Could be one-shot-only stuff." I held the scrap of paper over the candle, about three inches off the tip of the flame. The paper flared and exploded with a soft *whoosh!*

"Son of a whore," I bellowed. I slammed my other hand down on the table and upset the candle. The barest corner of paper was gripped in the tweezers now—the rest gone to hell.

Bud was shaking his head. Alicia said, "Guess that's that, yes?" She almost looked pleased; or maybe "relieved" was the better word to describe her expression.

"Guess so," I said. "So far as the treasure goes. On the other hand, the son of a bitch might have had something we can't even imagine written down on there."

Bud sat back, disconsolate. "We're fucked. I had been thinking about a hacienda somewhere on the coast of Baja."

"We're not necessarily through yet," I said, hiding my own disappointment. "This map stuff was apart from Prescott and the Skull and Bones. Remember—we've still got a good shot at secur-ing our eighty grand for turning Pancho's noggin here over to those assholes at Yale."

"True," Bud said.

Alicia sat down next to me and smiled uncertainly. "So we can skip this meeting with Holmdahl, yes?"

"Oh, God no," I said. "I don't think we should 'skip' that—not at all. There are some things to maybe learn there. And I haven't completely written off a treasure hunt. And I think that bastard Emil would like to know—should know—that Fierro is alive and in town. Part of me, maybe mostly the writer in me, would like to kick back and watch that knowledge put to some bloody end by Holmdahl. And hell, the ex-Cavalry part of me feels an obligation to maybe even throw in with Emil to take down Fierro. Maybe fulfill one of our old missions from the Expedition."

"You're *loco*," Alicia said. "Let those two old men kill one another if you will, but you stand back from it now. We mail this head off to your senator friend, get our money, and go back to our lives. That's my vote. Meet Holmdahl if you will, yes—just to point him at Fierro. But then end this before it truly harms one of us, Héctor. I mean, harms us beyond aching ribs, bleeding kidneys, black eyes and broken knuckles. Look at the two of you. What will *Señor* Holmdahl think when he gets a look at both of you with your limps and slow and careful ways of sitting down … with your swollen, barked knuckles and bruised faces and throats and your split lips?"

I looked at Bud and raised my eyebrows. It was long-pants time, now. The poet searched my eyes a minute and then nodded decisively. "The lady is right. Let's see Holmdahl, then make the contact with the senator and wrap this mess up."

Truth be told, I was inclined their way—but I feigned disappointment that I didn't feel. For some reason, I felt an obligation to play to character. "As we're still in a democracy," I said with a false edge, "you two win."

I leaned over and picked up the notepad. I took my fountain pen from my pocket and made a shopping list. I folded a couple of twenties up in the piece of paper and handed it to Bud. "We passed that grocery on the corner. How's about you two get some provisions?"

Alicia took the list from Bud and scanned it. She said, "Flour? Food coloring? We baking?"

"Yeah. Just desserts," I said. "We need to mock up a replacement skull for Emil. We'll use the food coloring and flour to put a good, fake welt on phony Pancho, here." I cocked my thumb at the fake skull with the biggest underbite.

I placed the piece of paper I'd cut from the notepad onto a cookie sheet, slid it into the range and turned up the gas on it for a minute. I pulled it out and inspected it. It looked a hundred years old now. It was a good facsimile of the slip of the treasure map I'd just inadvertently incinerated. I handed it to Bud along with a toothpick. "Keep these safe and at hand," I told him. "The time to employ those poetic gifts of yours is swiftly coming."

Fiske looked wary. "How so?"

"Once we talk to Emil, I hope that we're going to have a better handle on what we need to write on that scrap of paper in order to fool the old bastard." I pointed at the bathroom. "You'll have to do those honors, Bud. I would, but I'm pissing blood."

Bud smiled and said, "It's not my usual medium, you know."

22

WHILE Alicia and Bud shopped, I stashed Pancho's skull and the other head—the one we would pass off on Emil as the real thing when we had it ready—in the hall closet. I drank several glasses of water and fiddled with the dial on the radio until I found a border station. A mariachi band played "The Texas River Song," an old tune believed written by a long-dead teacher:

There's many a river
That waters the land
Now the fair Angelina
Runs glossy and gliding
The crooked Colorado
Runs weaving and winding
The slow San Antonio
Courses and plains
But I never will walk
By the Brazos again

All that water I had drunk down had its intended effect and I headed to the head. There was a good deal less blood in the bowl than I had anticipated. I'd steer clear of the liquor a few more days to be sure.

I ordered a couple of pizzas and a carton of Coca-Cola for delivery and hit the shower.

I dried off and dressed, and found Bud and Alicia already eating my pizza. I grabbed a couple of slices and wrapped them in a napkin and then holstered my Colt and slipped on my sports jacket. I picked up my parcel of pizza and told my partners I'd be back soon.

Bud chewed and swallowed and said, "What are you doin'?"

"Phone calls. Appointments."

"Can't call from here?" Alicia asked.

"Can't risk a phone trace. I'm keeping these calls short and sweet—and a good ways away from our dear Fortress of Solitude, here."

* * *

I wolfed down my pizza as I walked four blocks to a phone booth. I thumbed through the phone book and found a listing for what I deduced to be Holmdahl's stepdaughter's place. A woman, the stepdaughter, likely, answered. She went to fetch the old man. I waited, then a voice said, "Emil speakin'." It was good to hear another Texas accent.

"We go back, *amigo*," I said. "My name is Hector Lassiter."

"I've read your books, a few of 'em anyhows. You lookin' to write about me? Seems there's always some reporter or biographer comin' around these days. Can't say as I'm much interested."

"Uh, *no*. Me neither, truth to tell. I was there, riding with Pershing and you way back then. I've got my own memories for memoirs if I were inclined that way. And I so ain't."

"You were in the Expeditionary force?" Emil was palpably skeptical.

"That's right," I said. "We talked a few times. Shared a few drinks together. Shared our thoughts. And we shared at least one Mexican whore, I think."

"Guess that last makes us something."

"I'd like to think so."

"So, you lookin' to relive old times together, or something? Talk about stale tail? If so, I ain't frankly interested in that, neither. I keep movin' ahead. Never look back or dwell in the past—just kills you quicker."

"Drive on, huh?"

"That's it exactly," the old campaigner said. "Life is short, but *wide*, and I mean to pack mine full to burstin'."

I had to smile. I said, "In that spirit, I'm gonna cut to the chase. I have Pancho Villa's rotting head. And I know all the tales about you and treasure, tied, so to speak, to his fucking skull. I'm willing to deal for a cut of the gold and silver you recover. I'm no prospector myself, you see, but as I have his head …"

Emil snorted softly. "If I had a nickel for every time some yahoo has come to me with an old skull and a proposition.… Have to confess, though, you're the first guy who hasn't asked me to pay for the head up front."

"Well, the head's not for sale," I said. "See, I have other ambitions along those lines. I'm not going to give you the head, per se. I'm just gonna let you retrieve something you hid inside of that rotting bastard."

I could hear the excitement and terror in his voice now. "Have you looked that something over? Don't lie to me—I'll know."

"Hell no. Just looked enough to determine there's something you rigged that seems to run into the right eye. Can hear it shake around in there a bit. But I haven't gone further. Figure it couldn't possibly be that easy, Emil."

"You'd be right, Hector."

Hmm. Swapping first names—we were getting downright chummy.

"Here's my vision," I said. "I bring the head over, you take your little trinket from out of it, we strike a deal on your recovery, and I take the head away with me," I said.

"Gonna sell it to Yale, ain'tcha?"

"Maybe something like that."

"Won't even ask what you stand to get for it," Emil Holmdahl said. "On the one hand, it would probably depress me. On the other hand, it's academic, 'cause that cocksucker Pres Bush will dick you, just like he dicked me, I expect. In his current position, he could screw you big time. Worse than he ever did me."

"I'm doing my best to see he doesn't."

"Good luck with that, buddy. A fiction writer versus the U.S. intelligence services? I don't like your odds, *mi amigo.* So, you bringing that head my way now, then?"

"No can do. Looking to get some information, first."

Emil laughed. "You can't get enough from me to read the map, if that's your idea."

Map … damn.

"That's not my idea," I lied. "Thing is, since I got my hands on the head, a lot of bad things have been happening. So far, most of it has happened to other people, but I've had my brushes and enjoyed my share of dumb luck. I've survived long enough to know that luck can't run my way forever. Lot of dead people around me suddenly. And there's someone else wants Pancho's skull."

"Besides Bush, you mean?"

"Brace yourself: Rodolfo Fierro is still alive," I said. "This morning he nearly shot me to death outside a diner here in Los Angeles. You'll see it in the newspapers this afternoon. It's already on the radio, although they are reporting it as gang violence."

"So, Fierro found you." It was a simple statement on the old man's part. "And you didn't fucking kill him?"

No statement there—more like mocking accusation. Shaking my head, I said, "I have to say, I'm surprised you don't sound surprised to hear that Rodolfo is still north of the dirt. You must be the only guy from back then who doesn't believe *el Carnicero* drowned decades ago down there in the quicksand bog."

"I've heard stories to that effect for years," Emil said. "So, no, I'm not too surprised." The old mercenary paused, then said, "I'd love to see him a *last* time." He paused. "But you didn't fucking try to kill the Butcher yourself?" That was a direct accusation. One I let pass.

"Oh, I gave it a shot," I said. "Then the cops blundered onto the scene. Absent the intrusion of the fucking LAPD, he'd be stinking just fine now."

"Well, partner, you best keep your head down and yourself alive—least ways until I can have that session with Pancho Villa's head," Holmdahl said. "Come on by my place here and—"

"Don't be daft, Holm. I'm thinking more about a good chat, first. A chat some place public, where I can't be ambushed. Not ambushed by you or yours, mind you," I rushed to say, though I certainly wouldn't put a double-cross past him; on the contrary, I was planning for it. "You know what I mean—I don't want Bush's cronies or frat boys or Fierro and his *banditos* cornering me anywhere semi-private. That said, my friends and I will meet you at Aero Squadron tomorrow at ten a.m. Breakfast is on me."

"Your 'friends'?" Emil snorted again. "Gonna gang up on me, huh?"

"I doubt that we could do that."

"Me too. Tomorrow at ten a.m. then," Emil said. "Oh, and Hector, don't you go and die on me 'tween now and then, got it, *hombre*?"

"Promise, *amigo*. Honest Injun."

One down.

I took out my little notepad and flipped to Senator Bush's number. No guts, no glory.

23

THE senator kept it short and very spooky—in a CIA kind of way—all symbolic code-talk and mysterious mumbo-jumbo.

Bush said, "You have the parcel?"

I responded, "The all-important fucking 'parcel' is accounted for, *sí*. Empty eye sockets and remaining whiskers intact. All the attendant bullet holes are there. So, yes, Senator, your precious fucking skull is back in play."

"Don't use my title, please," Senator Bush said. "Or my name. I'm sure you're on an unsecured line."

"I'm sure you're sure that I am. Well, what the fuck should I call you, *amigo*?"

"Poppy."

Oh Christ. That nearly did it for me, right there.

I said, "No way, *hombre*. Fuck you and your Yale secret society. Fuck 'em all sideways. I've got my own handle for you. I'm gonna call you … 'Headhunter.' As a nod to poor Geronimo, you skull-thieving asshole."

"Please, *stop*—you're already making me hate you," the prissy senator said.

"Really? Well, it saves a step. You're gonna get there eventually anyway, so why not do it now?"

"This isn't the way we should proceed, Mr. Lassiter."

"Oh, Holy Jesus—*screw* this. I'm not going to go the cloak-and-dagger, hand-job route with you, your Honor. Just tell me true, eighty grand still the going price for a dead Mexican legend's head?"

I could envision the thin lips saying the words: "Presuming you can provide provenance? Then, yes." The senator sniffed.

"Provenance?" I almost snorted. "That ain't gonna happen. We both know that, Hoss. Sucker's been dead longer than your shot-down, World War II-ace son has been alive. And Villa's head has been bouncing around in limbo a very, very long time. Poor old Pancho, he's frankly the worse for wear. I don't have papers of authenticity. We both know that. We both accept that. My proof—my fucking 'provenance'—is just this big fucking underbite and a steadily growing pile of bodies."

There was a sharp intake of breath. Apparently, the career politician didn't like my use of the word "fucking." But what of the bodies? Well, cadavers, based on the evidence of Geronimo's headless torso, weren't much of an issue for this callous, blue-blooded character.

The senator said, "Bring the parcel on up to Connecticut, won't you? When you reach my town, call, and I'll send intermediaries to greet you. They'll take the parcel off your hands and you'll be paid your bounty."

"Please," I said. "You insult my intelligence. I'm not going down that path, no way, no how. We're going to use 'cut-outs,' to resort to your sad-ass spy parlance. And you're gonna make the first crucial leap of faith, *mi amigo*. You're going to pay eighty grand to a Swiss account of my choosing. I'll wire you the details *mañana*. The guy who will be bringing you the head is an *hombre* I think you're well acquainted with—Emil Holmdahl. When I see my account has been filled, then you'll get the rotting skull for your jerk-off Yale secret society."

"Very well," the senator said. He didn't sound too happy. And that gladdened my dark heart.

I said, "Here is my heartfelt advice, dumbass. You try and learn to *love* this plan, cocksucker. You *really* don't want to meet me face-to-face, you pinched-faced head thief. Just trust me on that."

The senator, just before hanging up and thus insuring himself the irrelevant last word, said, "Based on your violent and sorry excuse for novels, I suspect that's too terribly true, Mr. Lassiter."

24

I began the walk back to our new bungalow. There was a crack of thunder, then a warm and steady rain began falling. With hunched shoulders, I trotted through an alley to a side street that afforded a near-constant procession of storefront canopies leading back to my current digs.

One canopy was emblazoned with the name of an osteopath. For a fifty, the mercenary doc agreed to give me a cursory once-over.

I confided to the doc my fears regarding diabetes. He listened to my anecdotes and nodded gravely.

He checked my most recent wounds—deftly jerking the bandages from the backs of my hands before I could react. He leaned in close and clicked his tongue.

"When exactly were you wounded?" The doctor's brow furrowed as he examined the scratches on the backs of my hands.

I told him. He shook his head and "tsked-tsked."

My new doctor shook his head and looked me in the foggy eye. "These wounds should be much better healed than they are. They're a sorry sign, all on their own, I'm afraid. Those and the foot pains you describe. Though those could be from dehydration, too. You should drink more water every day. And as regards circulation, you strike me as an active man. We wouldn't want to lose our toes or our feet, would we?"

"We wouldn't."

The sawbones spiked me and drew my blood. Then he passed me a cup and asked me to hit the restroom and to piss into it. I said, "I will, but I'll warn you in advance, there may be some blood in there."

"You suspect you have a cancer?"

"No," I said. "Some son of a bitch punched me in the kidney."

My doctor-for-hire didn't blink. He scoped my bruised and swollen knuckles. He said, "I'll confess that I've read many of your books, Mr. Lassiter. I didn't realize until now that they were nonfiction." I reckoned he fancied himself a comedian, but down deep, I had a grudging affection for my accidental doctor for that crack.

The sawbones ran me through an eye test and then, frowning, he referred me to an optometrist two doors down. I took that as another grave sign.

"It'll be a few days before I have anything definitive in terms of your tests, but I think I can safely say I'm soon going to be prescribing insulin," the doctor said. "Stay away from sugar in the meantime and refrain from alcohol. Can you do that?"

I shrugged. "What exactly makes you think I couldn't?"

"It's the alcohol that concerns me."

I bit my lip, then said, "What makes you think I drink?"

My new doctor blinked and smiled politely. Then he blinked a few more times.

"I'll do my best to stay dry," I promised.

"I know you'll try for me. But you need to do this for yourself. That's what concerns me."

I patted his arm. "Don't confuse me with my characters."

"That's good advice. You should listen to yourself, Mr. Lassiter."

25

MY vision was fuzzy and my pupils light-sensitive from being dilated by the eye doctor as I resumed my walk back to Alicia and Bud. The rain had slowed to a soothing drizzle.

Fucked up as my vision was, I nevertheless sensed I had a shadow.

This fella in a black suit and tie fell in step behind me. He stood out on the Los Angeles streets in that dark and severe rig of his. I guessed him for FBI.

Soon enough, he laced arms with me and said, "Don't react. I'm Special Agent Duane David."

I smiled and shook loose my arm. "My strong sense is that you're just a Fed by title. But whose creature are you *really*, Duane? J. Edgar's, or do you do the bidding of Bush?"

He sneered and reached under his jacket. I felt a barrel dig into my ribs. "That's some kind of record," the alleged FBI agent said, "pissing me off this quickly."

"Yeah, well fuck you, Duane. If that's so, you're so far out of your league I can't help but feel for you."

He steered me to a food stand that was sculpted to look like a giant hot dog. We took up a table in the shade of the giant wiener. As we hadn't ordered any food, we drew cross looks from the fella manning the stand. "Duane"—a blond asshole in a too-tight black suit jacket—flashed his FBI identification. The proprietor flashed Duane his middle finger. Duane started to rise. The proprietor raised his other hand. He curled his lip and said, "You and fucking HUAC wrecked my uncle."

"Well, fuck you," Duane shot back.

"Making friends everywhere you go, huh?" I shook my head. "Screw this. *My* time is valuable. You arrest me, or you tell me what you want, or I'm gonna take the side of hot dog boy there. I'll start working my persuasive mouth and see you gutted by the resulting crowd."

Duane leaned in. "Don't fuck with me Lassiter. We have a file on you thicker than the hard-on I have for you, cocksucker."

Oh boy. This was calamitous strategy on his part. Now *I* had a hard-on. I said, "I'm thinking your 'thicker than' equals my invisible, *pendejo*. Again, my question stands. Exactly whose stooge are you, dumbass?"

Duane bit his lip. His fists were clenched and his cheeks were red. Good. The boy had a temper. He snarled, "I'm not going to fuck with you. You were prematurely anti-fascist, and—"

"Hey, Duane-O, fuck you and your slut mother. Think about that term all you FBI cocksuckers seem so warm to: 'prematurely anti-fascist.' What's that make you Johnny-come-latelys? *Tardily* anti-fascist? Can only be the term for it. Wanna know what else? I went over to Spain to raise money just to chase Spanish tail. I ain't a political animal."

"I should clap iron on you now."

"And I should put a bullet in your right eye and call your mincing boss and tell him you're schlepping for sorry-ass Yale. I'm right, aren't I?"

"Fuck you."

"I'm gonna take that as a 'yes.'" I stood and flipped the bird at Duane. I said, "You're out-gunned. Here's the thing, Duane—you come at me again, and I'll kill you. Fed or no."

"You're threatening a federal agent?" His face was red. His hand was trembling—wanting to stray to his gun, I guessed.

I leaned in close. I smiled, my lips and eyes close to his. "No, Duane. I'm threatening a card-carrying member of the Skull and Bones Society. And I think, push comes to shove, Hoover would side with me. I know how much J. Edgar likes running his own show. Hell, garbage men in Illinois know that. I'd wager if I make one or two phone calls up the chain, I can have you unemployed in under two minutes."

26

I'D nearly made it "home" when the second FBI agent accosted me. "I'm Special Agent Kenneth Brown. Spare me a moment, Mr. Lassiter?"

I stopped and turned. "You work with Duane David?" I glared at the fella and said, "I really have to think so. So, you know, I think I'm gonna say, respectfully, 'Fuck you,' agent."

Special Agent Ken Brown smiled. He said, "Me and Agent David, we're only titular partners, Mr. Lassiter. That's all."

I looked him over. This guy was slender as hell. White hair; a good smile. He held out his hand and I shook it.

"That's all?" I asked.

"That's all."

"Seems maybe enough," I said, curious now where this was headed.

Brown tipped his head to one side. "I'm frankly taking your measure, sir. I'm sure you're doing the same, sir. But I have an advantage. I've read *Wandering Eye*. I loved *Border Town*. Hell, I love *The Land of Dread and Fear*. I think it's your best book.

I frankly think I understand you and what matters to you, Mr. Lassiter. I've spent some time with Mr. Hoover's files on you. And I think, at base, maybe you and me are kindreds. So I'm going to gamble here. I'm going to confess that I have a pretty firm handle on what you're involved in. I think I know what you possess. If you don't know already, I'm going to say it up front: Agent David was recruited by the Bureau during his senior year at Yale. We now suspect another agency got to him first. We think Agent David is playing a double game. We think this because he was a member of the Skull and Bones Society. Please, Mr. Lassiter, don't insult my intelligence by pretending to act as if you don't know what I'm talking about. I'm certain you do. We've wired your car, put multiple tracers in it. To your credit, you quickly found one of those and sent several other agents—two of whom, parenthetically, are Skull and Bones members—to Idaho. But we correctly guessed once you found one tracer, you wouldn't look for redundant units."

"You bastards," I said.

"I can see how you could see it that way," Agent Brown said. "To be honest, we've traced every call you've made since you left New Mexico. We've even disposed of some bodies you or others left in your wake in order to shield you from various local law enforcement agencies and media outlets."

My head was spinning. I said, "For that, I guess I must say that I'm grateful."

"You should be," Agent Brown said. "I don't mean that in a gloatful sense, Mr. Lassiter. I just mean, well, you've collected some powerful enemies. The Skull and Bones are knitted tightly to the CIA and to the Secret Service, as I'm sure you know. That, frankly, concerns Mr. Hoover. I confide this to you at some personal peril. Particularly in so far as it concerns Special Agent Duane David. Mr. Hoover, understandably, can't abide CIA incursion into the

Bureau, even if said-agent David is acting primarily under the aegis of Yale secret society fealty."

I laughed and shook my head. "Jesus, you sound like a lawyer from hell."

Special Agent Brown shrugged. "I happen to have a law degree. For liability reasons, my verbiage regarding that particular nuance was required to be a rote recitation of agency-hired attorneys. 'Tween us, it disgusts me, too—wordy cocksuckers."

Someday, I thought, all the litigating assholes would accidentally destroy the world. And the CIA and FBI and their constant attempts to out-dick one another would result in bloodshed of epic proportions.

I steered Agent Brown back to the CIA mess.

"Fucking CIA, they're foreign, aren't they?" I shook my head and said, "They're not remotely domestic, right? At least by design, they can't operate on U.S. soil? So far as J. Edgar is concerned, they're over-reaching their charter by nosing around the domestic front, yeah?"

Special Agent Brown stared hard at me. He was really taking my measure, now. "That's essentially accurate, yes, sir. But they are also fucking with Mr. Hoover's agency. Mr. Hoover can't countenance rogues pissing in his pond. Sir."

"Now you're speaking my language, Agent Brown."

He shook loose a cigarette from a soft pack and I accepted it. He shook loose a second for himself. I fired us both up with my Hemingway Zippo. "The rest has to be off the record," the FBI agent said. "The director would gut me for going where I'm about to go, sir. Do you understand? I need my job. I have two daughters to support. I need you to handle this information with real discretion."

"Sure," I said. "I get that. Thee and me, Agent Brown, we have made a separate peace. By the way, if I'm being watched by David and his cronies, aren't you worried you'll be spotted here with me?"

"You're on light surveillance currently, as we have your car wired and your phone tapped. You've established what appears to be a domicile with your two friends. You're easily found. For the moment, it's just me and Agent David tailing you. Agent David who needed a haircut. I threatened to report him to our superior. Director Hoover is very, very fussy about our appearance, as I'm sure you know. So Agent David is now at a barbershop."

"'Fussy'?" I smiled. "One must be fastidious in his sartorial presentation, yes."

"I hate it too," Agent Brown said. "And now who sounds like a goddamned lawyer? But there's another reason your security is light."

"I'm all ears, Agent," I said.

"You'll be accumulating additional surveillance in a very short time," Brown said. "When you meet with Mr. Holmdahl, two investigative lines will be crossing. I hope you understand I'm breaking a confidence sharing this with you."

"Mum's the word." I said, "You're already watching Holmdahl?"

"For many, many years now, yes," Agent Brown said. "We—well, actually the Secret Service—first questioned Holmdahl in 1952 regarding twenty million in gold he was reputed to have smuggled out of Mexico."

"Villa's gold?"

"Perhaps. But more likely, not. We think Holmdahl is also searching for Villa's gold. He's made several trips to the Las Nieves region—Durango—where Villa's gold is still rumored to be hidden. This other twenty million is something else … maybe something foreign—in a dark sense."

Jesus … maybe Emil was more mercenary than even I knew.

Agent Brown slipped me a sheet of paper. "A special phone number. Call it if you need to. You'll be in touch with me within five minutes."

27

THE night before a battle—that's what it felt like, anyway.

The whole escapade was starting to remind me of one of my own novels from the late-1940s.

Overlapping and conflicting objectives. Third and fourth parties hiding private agendas.

The looming specter of double- or triple-crosses.

If I were plotting it, I would find a way to have Duane and Emil screw one another, to have Fierro wind up dead. Bud and me would end up with a king's ransom and "I" would get the girl. At least for the short term. All my books seem to end in death—never any happy endings.

Just like life.

But, hell, maybe I could "plot" it after all, manipulate events toward some end of my own.

I found myself a table in a dark corner of the tavern. I ordered a club sandwich and a bottle of club soda, took out my notebook and tried to write while I waited for my food.

I didn't really have a story I could get going, so I started writing descriptions of Alicia, depicting her in different settings and situations. I tried to imagine what her mannerisms would be and what she would say in certain circumstances. Those descriptions and fragments of dialogue eventually began to spread out into a short story about a young, unwed Mexican mother sleeping with an older and doomed *Villista* the night before his final battle.

Roman à clef? Push come to shove, I'd surely be hard-pressed to deny it.

The tavern had a small stage and a good sound system. Two guys with guitars were strumming and belting out cowboy tunes and border ballads. I didn't know most of the tunes and so figured they must be original compositions. But they were riveting and authentic. The singer/songwriter was this prematurely white-haired dude who introduced himself as "Buddy Loy Burke." He wore dark-tinted glasses and a white straw cowboy hat. Dude had a dry sense of humor and a riveting baritone. His accompanist was tall and skinny and a genius on the guitar. The singer was crooning a tune about lost romance and resulting regrets that he called "The Ones That Got Away"—a pitilessly self-appraising border ballad that cut straight to my black and bloodied heart.

My club sandwich came and I ate and drank soda water and coffee and listened to the singer … stealing occasional thirsty glances at the glasses of whiskey and bourbon gripped in the hands of the other patrons seated around me.

I finished eating, wrote for the duration of another four or five songs, and then felt fingertips trail across the back of my neck. I looked up and Alicia smiled and leaned over and kissed my mouth. "Am I interrupting?" She nodded at my notebook. "I'd understand if you said yes."

"No. You're not. I'm finished. Have a seat and I'll buy you a drink and stare lustfully. At the drink and at you, I mean. And not necessarily in that order."

She smiled and nodded. She pointed at the singer. "He's quite wonderful. I requested a song for you. One Bud says you favor: 'Tramps & Hawkers,' but with what Bud called, 'the Jim Ringer lyrics.'"

"Seems Bud knows me better than I do." I smiled and squeezed her hand. "It's probably my favorite tune. How in hell did you find me?"

She smiled. "It's the closest bar in walking distance."

I almost winced, but said, "I haven't gotten to apologize to you for that stuff with Bud the other day, Alicia."

"'Alicia,'" she repeated. "So ... *poised*. But you needn't be, you know." Alicia brushed a black wing of hair back from above her left eyebrow and smiled. "Forget it. Bud explained for you."

"Explained how much?"

"Enough. Enough that I can link it to things I've heard from Miss Dietrich, and from Mr. Welles. And things I have deduced to make me think I know all of it. Or at least as much as I want or need to know about how it was."

I started to speak, but couldn't figure out anywhere to go with it. I wanted to say, "And knowing what you think you know, you can sit here with me? Perhaps even stay with me?"

Alicia carefully stroked the bruise fading under my eye from where Bud had belted me. "Maria—your woman—she failed you," she said. "But worse, that woman failed your little girl ... in so many terrible ways."

My new favorite troubadour was singing "Prairie in the Sky" now—a wickedly beautiful ballad seasoned with imagery of big skies and dying sunsets and desert birds taking wing.

I said, "Whatever she did, it could never excuse what I did." I hesitated. "Do you need more from me? I've never really talked about it. But I would tell you, if you wanted ... in spite of every-thing it could cost me."

"No," Alicia said, shaking her head. "No, Héctor. I know enough about what I think happened. If it is of any consolation, I would have maybe done it myself under similar circumstances. The men who raped me ... I think I could have killed them. Or at least maimed them. Understand—I love my daughter. But I would kill the men who gave her to me. So I understand these bloody thoughts you have ... and maybe acted on."

"Can you live with them? Live with me, and my having had them?"

"I'm not sure yet. Perhaps not." She sighed and her fingers traced my mouth. "Is it always like this being with you? Running and ducking and fighting to survive?"

"Not exactly like this."

"But *usually*, you're saying. Close enough, in other words ... you writer. Because you like it like this. That could be a problem for us." She squeezed my hand and began moving our joined hands in time to the music. "When this is over—this of the heads—what do you do then, Héctor? Do you go on to the next bit of mayhem? Do you crawl into some bottle and start dying again? What do you propose to do?"

My Mexican darling certainly pulled no punches. Down deep, I adored her for her candor. The women who can really lay a glove on me are always the ones I'm most a fool for. Alicia was the quick-est study I'd yet crossed.

I lied, "I don't think that far ahead, these days."

"You should. You should think about the future ... and what form it might take for you."

"Marlene told me back there in Venice that I don't have any more future."

Alicia smiled and looked up at me with bedroom eyes from under her black bangs. Her hand was warm in mine. "Well, you have no prospect of one with her, that much is certain," she said. "And she's merely a Hollywood actress: what can a narcissist such as she possibly know of anything that matters? You know what Hollywood women are like."

"But you're trying to be what she is."

"I just want to support my daughter," Alicia said. "I'm only interested in giving her a good life and in seeing that she goes to school so she can make her own way. That's all ... it's a means to an end." Alicia smiled a tired smile. "You want to go 'home' now?"

I smiled and stroked her cheek. "Soon. But, for a time, can we just sit here and hold hands and listen to this guy sing?"

Alicia smiled sadly and squeezed my hand. She scooted her chair around close to mine and curled into my arm, her head resting on my shoulder and her hand tapping time on my thigh as the troubadour began to sing "my song" about rambling: blinding sun and snow; mountains and oceans; gypsies; ghosts and lost darlings; and the San Joaquin—the most beautiful and wonderful goddamn place I've found on this increasingly sorry planet.

I said, "I don't really want to die you know."

Alicia twisted her head around. We locked gazes. Her dark eyes were glistening.

"No," she said after a time. "I don't think you care a bit about dying. What you really don't want is to grow old."

28

I rose early and wrote for three hours—fleshing out the story I had started that was centered on Alicia. I could taste her on my mouth; the smell of her and us together clung to me. I started coffee and grabbed the *Los Angeles Times* from the front stoop. I flipped through it and found a review for my current novel, *The Land of Dread and Fear.*

The book reviewer, this little pilot fish called Lee G. Todd, agreed the title of my novel was "well-chosen." He said it was so because he "feared" my novel was terrible and it filled him with "dread" of any more books from me.

I could envision the little hack eunuch at his typewriter, wringing his hands with glee over that one.

Lee savaged my novel. But his barbs and attacks were wrapped in too-carefully constructed prose and smarmy little sarcasms that screamed of more "creative" self-congratulation.

My book wasn't the anchor for the piece.

The so-called reviewer's reaction to my novel didn't come across as the pivot for the review, either.

This was all about the reviewer preening and prancing and playing to his presumed reader. And making a name for himself by tearing down a bigger man—a real writer.

My book was a means to some twisted end whose true nature was known only to Lee and me. But it made my blood boil. "Lassiter can usually be counted upon to move matters along in a pulpy and peppy fashion,"—(*peppy*?)—"but here he stalls out as he partners his aging, bitter *gringo* with a Mexican pin-up who couldn't exist outside of a narcissistic, old crime writer's fetid imagination."

Mr. Lee G. Todd said my descriptions of *La Frontera* "bogged down the action" and the perceived "romance" derailed my "otherwise competent, if not particularly original, mystery story." He wrote that chapter nine smacked of a sense of a "writer clearly trying to write above himself."

The diseased bastard said I should take lessons in mystery writing from Dame Quartermain.

Mystery writing?

I've never written a "mystery" in my life. I'm a *crime* writer.

Lee said the "clipped and hyper-stylized" prose that I'd employed kept "getting between" him "and the story." He said that my prose style "kept reminding" him that he was "reading a book."

Huh. Me, I'm *always* aware I'm reading a book when I'm, well, *reading a book.*

But then the bastard really crossed the line. He dismissed any notion of "persona" and went and confused me with my protagonist. He said I was my "own worst-invented character." And *then* he mentioned my dead wife and child. He implied the plot was calculated "to vent some sense of guilt the author might be experiencing … to deflect some terrible culpability."

I tore the paper into pieces and beelined for the phone book to look for his address. I would kill the bastard with my bare hands—let my fists "get between him" and the rest of his sorry fucking excuse for a life.

Then I calmed down a bit, going cold inside like I always do before setting in motion terrible things that scare me later. I assessed angles.

I dug through my wallet and found the number for my friend "Packy" Thompson. Packy was an old boxer who'd found the bottle and reluctantly but effectively transitioned into contract work for Mickey Cohen and other Left Coast takers.

I dialed and found he was living in L.A. He gave me an address where I should leave the money—a "dead drop."

I was just closing the deal when Bud came in.

"No," I said to the aging former boxer, "just his hands. That'll be enough, Pack."

Bud gestured at the phone as I hung up. "What was that about?"

"Just responding to a critic."

29

GET a look at Emil Holmdahl: a crisply-pressed, starched checkered shirt buttoned all the way up and accented with a black and silver bolero tie, lizard-skin boots and khaki jodhpurs. He cinched those crazy pants with a hand-tooled, turquoise-studded belt and carried a Stetson in his callused hand. His shock of full, white hair was brushed neatly back from a high forehead. After all the years and the picaresque living Emil had packed in since I'd known him, I expected him to look older.

We shook hands. The old man had a good grip on him.

Not for the first time, I wondered if Emil suffered from a mild strain of dwarfism. He'd always had a horse face and arms too long for his body. Age had exaggerated his asymmetry. Emil's shoulders were now narrow and sloped and his torso seemed even more strangely stunted. What height he had always seemed to reside between his waist and knees. His lower legs were too short and the brown cowhide boots he affected now didn't make 'em look much longer, though I suspected he thought they did—no other way to justify wearing those things out in L.A. in 1957. He looked like a George Rozen pulp magazine cover in those damned boots, whose heels probably gave him an extra inch, and yet got him nowhere near proportional.

Holmdahl had a few years on me, but I sensed maybe that that morning, anyway, I looked older, more tired.

Alcohol withdrawal—now of all times—couldn't be helping much on that front.

And those of us who truly live in our heads seem to age harder. Probably the booze and the cigarettes and late nights and the whoring. Or not enough of those things to kill us while we are young and beautiful.

The soldier of fortune gave Bud a bemused once-over and a perfunctory handshake.

The courtly old bastard bowed and kissed Alicia's hand.

He glanced over and said to me, "I remember you now." His saying it gave me chills.

We went inside the Aero Squadron, with all its old military artifacts, and were led to a backroom I'd paid extra for where we could talk about things like lost treasure and stolen heads and grave-robbing.

Emil smiled at me. He said, "The head close by?"

The head—Emil was already rubbing me the wrong way. After all, he'd served under Villa for a time. It was bad enough he later turned on Pancho, but then to dig Villa up, saw off his head and stuff it with a map? Just what kind of sorry son of a bitch did it take to do all that? I shook my head, wondering how long I could hide the hatred that seeing Emil again stoked in me.

"Course not," I said. "And I sincerely hope you haven't done something stupid and obvious like have a confederate toss our place while we're meeting here."

"That would be too obvious, wouldn't it?" The old man waved his hand. "That would be amateurish. And it wouldn't engender trust when I didn't find it. I figure you've hidden it well. So, no, I ain't that stupid."

"Sure." Truth was, Pancho's head was in the trunk of my car, just outside. Not that it was that important an artifact now—now that we knew that I had accidentally torched the treasure map it once contained.

I said, "So that something you've got stashed in Pancho's head ... I figure it for a document. Invisible ink—something simple. What was it? Piss? Maybe lemon juice? Onion juice, or vinegar? Something like that, probably?"

Holmdahl snorted and shook his head. "Christ no. That's like something out of a pulp novel—no offense intended."

"None taken."

"Anyway, that's Boy Scout crap," he said. "I'm glad you didn't try heating the baby up. We used magician's flash paper. Sucker would have gone up, just like that. Glad you had the brains not to screw with it."

Alicia sipped her water, looking at me over the glass.

I shifted in my seat. "Me too," I said.

"I'll tell you what we used, and do it just because it won't help you anyway," Holmdahl said. "That map—hell, I've never seen its contents either. But I'll explain that part later. Thing is, you have to know exactly where to start in order to use the directions on the note."

"Tricky. And you know that place."

"I do. Just me, now. The other two guys who might have done something with it are dead."

Alicia set her glass down. She said, "Natural causes?"

Emil gave her a nasty smile. "As it happens, yes, dear. We wrote the note in ammonia with an eagle's quill. You reveal it with a light sponge wash of red cabbage water."

"Neat," Bud said.

Emil smirked. "Those new boots hurting you, boy? Oh, and it's impolite to keep your hat on indoors. Do that in Texas, and you'll get your ass kicked by an old lady."

Bud's cheeks reddened. "Thanks," he said. I'd firmly admonished my young poet to stay stoic and silent. I sure as hell didn't need Bud stirring Emil up with his angry remarks like he had that equally hair-trigger Yale pointdexter back at my hacienda.

Emil said to me, "Where'd you find this boy?"

"He's my ward," I said. "I'm mentoring him in the finer points of writing … and in living the kind of life that makes the muse open her legs."

"Interesting," Holmdahl said. He glanced at Alicia and back at me. "But coarse talk in front of a lady, Hector. Back in the forties, I read that book you wrote about the private eye and the Mexico City working girl—*Border Town*. I think the lad here's got a distance to go to reach your level of worldliness … and dissolution."

Now I found myself having to tamp down my own flaring anger. Or maybe Emil meant to say "disillusion." But probably not.

"I don't second-guess myself much these days, Emil," I said. "'Maybe in error, but never in doubt.' That's my motto."

Emil Holmdahl snorted and sipped his iced tea—no liquor for him. "My motto is: 'In God we trust; all others pay cash.'"

"It suits you," I said. "I mean, you hunted your old buddy Pancho for what, just money?"

"What else is there?" The old man gestured at my left side. "What do you pack?" The door to our dining room was closed. The waitstaff knew to knock before entering. I unholstered my Colt and pushed it across the table. The old man whistled and picked it up. "My God, a '73. She's a beauty." He turned her over, weighed her, ran his hands across her like he was stroking a woman's inner, upper thigh. He passed my gun back to me and pulled his own jacket back. "I'm a Mauser man, myself."

"Very nice," I said. "It's a C/96, yeah? A horseman's gun."

"Exactly. Ever done any time, Hector?"

"Not really. Slept off a few drunk and disorderlies in some of the better cities, but just overnight stuff."

"Didn't think so. You don't have the look."

"I know you've done your stints … for grave-robbing, for instance," I said. "And for violating neutrality laws."

Alicia wrinkled her nose. "What does that mean, to 'violate neutrality laws'?"

Bud Fiske smiled. He'd taken off his hat and stowed it on the seat of the empty chair next to him. "I'm going to take a stab and say gun-running."

Emil Holmdahl winked and touched his nose. "Right-o. Not as callow as you look, boy. Sentenced to eighteen months in the federal pen. Then Pancho raided Columbus, New Mexico—killed those civilians and bought himself a chase from Black Jack Pershing. They needed guides and I fit the bill. When you're in a spot like I was—prison—it always helps to have rare talents."

"But you never got us near enough to take a shot at Villa," I said. "No offense, but history is history. Or will you tell me you purposely fucked it up because of some lingering fondness for Pancho?"

"I still liked Villa well enough … but it was an impossible mission," Emil said. He spoke now to Alicia and Bud. "It was a crazy piece of business. Villa hurt us. Hit the U.S. in its own backyard. Killed civilians. So Wilson had to make Villa pay. But his response was ill-considered. Like everything else that cocksucker, blue-blood Woodrow Wilson did. Mark my words, son—never, ever serve in an army in a time of war under a president with no personal military service. And particularly under a Democrat—they don't know how to win wars."

Bud, who I sensed had a touch of leftist in him, said, "What about FDR … Truman?"

"Atom bomb," Holmdahl said. "Couldn't lose with that device in the mix. FDR died before he could steal defeat from the jaws of victory. And then Truman turned around and gave us Korea, where he couldn't drop the A-bomb. My analysis holds. But back to Villa—terrible logic there. Sending 10,000 men into Mexico to hunt down and murder a native son—a national hero to so many? That's bad judgment. It was only ever going to drive a wedge between us and Mexico. And we could have sent 100,000 men across the border and never found a single man who really wanted to hide in that desert country. They'd have been ahead to hire an assassin. In fact, I almost drew that duty."

This was news to me. I said, "Elaborate, wouldn't you?"

"Colonel Herbert Slocum—he personally made me the offer to go in and kill Villa," Holmdahl said.

I shrugged, hating Emil again. "Money is money to you. And you'd killed many men by then. You agreed to hunt Villa, why'd you say no to assassination?"

"Because it smacked of a suicide run, mostly," the old mercenary said. "I'm pretty attached to myself, having lived this long. And you know what? I actually did like Villa. I *personally* liked him. He was a good guy. A man's man. Even though I came to fight against him, I could never hate the magnificent bastard. He had some good qualities. And, hell, I'm a lot of things—many of them very bad—but I ain't no assassin. And, like I said, it was a suicide run—like those Japs in their Zeros, diving down at our boats. Yellow cocksuckers." Holmdahl blushed and smiled awkwardly at Alicia. "Pardon my French, please, *señorita*."

"It's okay," she said. My Mexican beauty pointed at me. "I've been around him a while now. I've learned all kinds of new vulgarities since meeting Héctor."

"I'm sure that's true," the old man said. "You're a man's woman, if you know what I mean. No better kind. Well, if I had killed Villa in Mexico, I would never have gotten out of the country alive to collect that money."

Bud, incorrigible Bud, couldn't hold back. "But it was alright to cut off the 'magnificent bastard's' head? To cut into and root around inside the skull of a man you knew and liked?"

To my surprise and relief, Emil took that one in stride. He looked Bud in the eye and answered him—giving me the sense he was warming to Bud in his own way. "That was different, son," Holmdahl said. "Villa was just rotting meat then. Everything that made Villa Villa was gone, fled to oblivion or Valhalla or wherever his kind finally flees to. Do you believe in an afterlife, Hector?"

I answered, too fast and too honestly. "Me, I don't harbor illusions of such things," I said. "I'm kind of counting on oblivion." I could feel Alicia's gaze on me. It didn't feel comforting. I wished I'd answered the old warrior more obliquely.

Alicia said, "What about you Mr. Holmdahl? Do you believe in heaven or hell, or both?"

"I gotta go with your beaten-up-on beau," the old man said. "If there is such a place as hell, I'm in a world of hurt, Beauty."

She said, "How is it Villa never came after you … I mean, after he was allowed to retire?"

Emil patted her hand. "I was on the move—overseas—a hard target to acquire. And hell, Mexico secured all kinds of assurances from Villa that he'd be a good boy if they let him live on his farm and fight cocks and bed women. He had to commit to doing nothing that would give the U.S. an excuse to come in again and get him. Killing an American, even one like me, was just not an option for Villa."

"Let's talk about the treasure," I said.

The old man smiled and leaned forward, crossing his too-long arms on the table. "Yes. Let's. That's what we all care about. And it's sure as hell more interesting than this jawing about afterlives."

"Let's talk treasure," I said again.

The old campaigner nodded. "I first heard about Villa's lost gold and Fierro's death when you'd likely heard it, I'd reckon along about 1915. I had some legal issues I was grappling with about then. Couldn't run right down to Durango to make my fortune. At the time, I was trying to avoid that quick stop from a short fall."

Alicia shot me a confused look. I said, "He means a noose."

"Ah," she said, stroking black hair behind her right ear.

"I heard the stories that I think many of us heard," the old mercenary said, looking at me. "Stories about Urbina, his betrayal of Villa and abandonment of the revolution. You know … that stuff. How Urbina holed up in Las Nievas, Durango with all that gold and silver. You probably know what happened next. Villa confronted his old friend at Urbina's ranch, then Pancho ordered Fierro, the Butcher, to kill Urbina. Even Villa didn't have the stomach to see his old friend die on his orders—particularly at the hands of a sadistic madman like Fierro. So Pancho left, and then the Butcher took Urbina apart, one piece at a time. After they finally killed him, they packed up the gold that they could carry and hid the rest. They split, and Fierro sank in that quicksand bog."

I leaned in now. "Yeah. That's the myth. But we now both know he didn't sink in the quicksand."

Bud chimed in, "And you, Mr. Holmdahl, didn't seem too surprised to learn Fierro is alive."

Emil Holmdahl shrugged and sipped some water. "You always heard stories. The one I kept hearing was that Fierro faked his death. He could take the measure of men pretty good, Rudy Fierro could. Particularly when he was sounding for treachery and hate in his underlings. Fierro gambled his own men wouldn't try to save him if he was in jeopardy, and, brothers and sister, was he ever proven right on that count."

"Please explain," Alicia said.

Holmdahl smiled and spoke directly to the young Mexican woman. "Fierro purposely rode into fast-moving, dangerous waters. He beelined for the one place along that *arroyo* you would purposely avoid if you were any kind of a horseman, and Fierro was certainly that. Yet Rudy rode right in. His horse began to flail. Fierro pretended to go under with her. Then he swam a ways and beached himself downstream, thinking he'd wait his flunkies out. Or so he thought. His plan, the story goes, was to return for the treasure they'd left behind."

Alicia asked, "He was going to betray Pancho Villa? After just executing another traitor?"

"It was money, honey," Holmdahl said. He ran his hand back through his thick, white shock of hair. "A lot of money. Rodolfo, he was no fool, you know. A stone killer, yes, but not stupid by any stretch. He could see the writing on the wall. The American government's fascination with Villa was wavering, due largely in part to Fierro's viciousness—all those mass shootings he had staged. And the politics were very … fluid. Do you know that saying the goddamned towel heads have? 'My enemy's enemy is my friend.' You know? Well, allegiances change … national agendas shift. It wasn't even a year later that it all got shot out from under Pancho by that stroke-enfeebled imbecile Woodrow Wilson. Wilson was choking off Villa's guns. So Pancho Villa seemingly retaliated against Wilson's and America's betrayal. On March 2, the raid on Columbus happened. A short time later, me and your beau and a bunch of others streamed across the border behind

Black Jack Pershing to bring Villa back, 'dead or alive,' as the dumbass saying goes. An Army of ten thousand; five hundred vehicles; eight biplanes; even George S. Patton, bossing us. Eleven months, four hundred miles, and squat."

Fiske lit a cigarette. By Christ, I'd addicted the poor, scrawny bastard. My tyro poet lit his cigarette with a hammered-nickel Zippo he'd seemingly picked up sometime in the last day or so. It looked as if it was engraved on one side. When Bud sat it down by his right hand, I scooped it up and tilted it until the light fell right. I read the opening line of my novel *Border Town*: "Whores Die Hard." Underneath, he'd had my name engraved.

Bud said, "I'm confused," as he reached over and took his lighter back from me. "Fierro stayed alive—we now know that's true—he knew where in Durango the treasure was hidden, but he didn't go back and get it. Why the hell didn't Fierro do that? Vengeful as he was, after you stole Pancho's head and tried to make off with the gold, why didn't Fierro come for you?"

Holmdahl smiled at Bud. "That's good listening, son—well, better'n I'd have given you credit for at first flush. And you're thinking, too. How'd this come to be, you ask me—Fierro knowing where to find the gold and silver, and yet not claiming it? Problem was, Fierro was too good a teacher ... well, in the sense that he ruled by absolute fear. He demanded excellence in a way no other son of a bitch ever has or will again. So, one of Rudy's own lieutenants—a young man of pride and conscience—spotted Fierro when he surfaced a ways downstream. He saw Rudy break surface and slide behind a stand of weed and willow there at the banks. That smart and sharp-eyed flunky of Fierro's correctly intuited what Rudy—the Butcher—was planning. The flunky dispatched several men to ride out and overtake Villa. Plan was for them to inform Pancho that Fierro had turned on Villa and the revolution—tell Pancho that Fierro was angling to rob *el Jefe* just like Urbina had. Then that old boy and another passionate and loyal, young Villista rode out in pursuit of Rodolfo Fierro."

"So way back then, Pancho, too, knew that Fierro survived," I said. "Guess he kept that sad-ass fact secret because two men that close to Villa trying to fuck him would smack of weakening leadership."

Emil gave me a nasty look and then jerked his head in Alicia's direction. "Watch your foul mouth around the lady, boy," he said.

Boy? "Sure," I said. "Sorry to offend *your* sensibilities. *Sir.*"

Emil said, "Exactly. That's exactly what it would have looked like. Loss of control. One lieutenant straying off the res'? Well, that can be dismissed as bad judgment. But two? In a week? That's an authority-threatening mudslide."

"Sure," Bud said. "That all makes sense. But here's the central thing: what kept Fierro from the treasure?"

"The initial pursuit, for one thing," Holmdahl said. "Rodolfo may have been packing guns after his faked drowning—hell, I suspect we can trust that he was. But the bloodthirsty bastard was still on foot—his horse having drowned in that damned bog."

"But Villa knew Rudy too well. When the larger body of men caught up with Pancho, and told him what Fierro was apparently trying to do, well, Pancho knew that a mere two men chasing Fierro didn't bode well. Villa sent ten men in as reinforcements to support the two poor bastards already chasing Fierro. The support crew rode maybe ten miles before they found the two dead Villistas. The sons of bitches had been stripped naked and staked out belly-down over maguey plants—impaled—and what was left, half-eaten by coyotes and ants."

Alicia arched a dark eyebrow. "How do you know this, sir? In such ... vivid detail?"

Holmdahl jacked a thumb in my direction. "Ask Lassiter. You heard things along the sweltering trail. We didn't have TV, didn't have radio … hell, not even newspapers. *Hell,* we didn't even have short-dogs—those funny-looking short and wide paperbacks they printed for the Grunts during World War II and Korea. We had gossip. *Corridos.* We had stories. You *heard* things out there in the alkali."

Okay. It was something like true. But you didn't hear things like *this.* Not with this level of novelistic detail. Two dead Villa loyalists; some other Villa faithful who rode out. That old bastard Homldahl was either embroidering, or obscuring. Or there was another, more chilling prospect—Holmdahl had heard it from one of the central players. But which one?

"Fierro had eaten one horse and rode off on the other," Emil continued. "For months, the reinforcement Villistas chased Fierro, or so the legends, which I credit, say. They drove the Butcher deeper into southern Mexico—back toward Sinaloa, where the monster was born. Try as he might, old Fierro just couldn't get back to Durango for months. Then Villa allegedly raided Columbus, apparently killed all those innocents—and the troops. And we all invaded Mexico—the so-called 'Punitive Expedition.' Nobody, but nobody, could move around in Mexico once we made the scene. Least of all Rodolfo Fierro, who had met Black Jack Pershing and who had appeared in some pretty famous photos with Villa and Pershing. And Fierro was well-known to all of us horse soldiers from wanted posters and such. You have to understand," Holmdahl said, speaking to Alicia and Bud now, "word of Fierro's 'death' in the quicksand bog got back to us well after the raid on New Mexico. And that raid was so brutal—so craven and so brazen—well, we all at first assumed Fierro probably master-minded the goddamned thing."

"Yeah, yeah," Bud said, clearly getting impatient. "But after you all left—after you were shipped off to Europe for the Great War—why didn't Fierro go back then? Go back and get that treasure?"

Emil smiled, rueful and proud, all at once. "Well," he said, "I got there first, boy."

30

HOLMDAHL took a couple of forkfuls of scrambled eggs, then asked me, "You ever hear of a fella name of Al Jennings?"

"Heh, sure," I said. "Grifter, actor, religious scam artist. 'The Last of the Great Train Robbers,' according to himself."

Alicia smiled. "Was he? The last of the great train robbers, I mean?"

"Naw, what he was is a horse's ass," I said. "First-class screwup. He and his band once tried to stop a train they had targeted. They tried to stop it by piling these jumbo-sized discarded tires on the tracks. The engineer flipped them the bird and opened up the throttle. When the train hit the tires, it tossed them thirty or forty feet in the air. When those big, heavy, rubber suckers started raining back down, well, Jennings and his crew nearly got killed by those damned tires."

"Right," Holmdahl said. "Then he hooked up with Bill Porter— William Sydney Porter—you know, the short-story writer, O. Henry? Jennings and Porter bungled some other crimes together and finally ended up in the penitentiary in Columbus—that's the city in Ohio, not the one in New Mexico that Villa attacked, by the way."

Bud tipped his chair back on two legs. "Are you saying you chose to hook up with this guy … even knowing what a joke he was?"

"Even a stopped clock is right twice a day," Holmdahl said. "Once in a while, Al'd get a line on something that held real promise. He and me and this other fella, a Texan named Jake Chrisman, well, we decided to form a partnership and go for Urbina's—Villa's—treasure. We had all heard the same stories and kind of tripped over one another's mutual preparations to go hunting the treasure. At that point, it seemed better to throw in together than to try and dick one another in order to get there first. Or at least it seemed politic to give the pretense of doing so.

"The fucking *federales* fell on us about four miles from Urbina's ranch." Emil suddenly blushed and smiled sheepishly at Alicia. "Now *I'm* talking dirty in front of you, *señorita*." The old man jerked his head at me and then grimaced. "I personally blame Lassiter's bad influence."

I glanced at Bud. My "interviewer" was on his third cigarette. Hard to argue with Holmdahl's assessment of the nasty and self-destructive effect I have on those closest to me.

"Anyways, the Mexican authorities killed three of our Mexican guards/guides," Holmdahl said. "The rest of us just barely escaped with our lives," he said, staring at the ceiling but clearly not seeing it. I sensed that Holmdahl was living in the back then, now. "Jennings went on back to Texas," Emil said. "Al was yellow to the core. But me and Chrisman, well, we figured two careful gringos on horseback would be a lot less conspicuous than that crew we went down there with the first time. So just the two of us returned to Urbina's ranch."

I thought of Al Jennings and said, "And a two-way split beats the hell out of splitting three or four ways."

Bud smiled and said, "Or eight or nine ways—once your praetorian guard figured out what was up if you'd reached the ranch that first time."

Emil Holmdahl shrugged. "Plan that time was to try and do it under their noses. We'd get the treasure, then move it to a safe place of our choosing, away from those characters' eyes and ears. Then, later, we'd come back and claim it. Or, if it seemed a better prospect, we'd have just killed them all once we had the treasure. We'd murder them without a second thought, knowing they'd do the same to us, tables turned. They were nasty pieces of work. And because of that, they wouldn't have been missed, let alone mourned. Probably wouldn't have prompted an investigation."

Alicia blinked in disbelief at Holmdahl's casual confession. Her cheeks reddening, she said, "I'm surprised you could sleep at night. I mean, in that I'd think you'd be looking for ways to off one another … have the gold without having to split with anyone else. How could you trust your associates? How could they trust you not to kill them, too?"

"I'd be a liar if I said the thought of taking them out didn't cross my mind, and many times, at that," Holmdahl said with bland sincerity. "And I'd be a fool to think that Al and Jake didn't suspect me of having thoughts about killing them. I sure figured they aimed to screw me in the end. So yes, missy, at some point, before we abandoned our first foray, it was looking to turn into some replay of *Treasure of Sierra Madre*—all of us looking over our shoulders at one another.

"But anyway, me and Jake lingered, then we went back and we found the treasure. It wasn't really at Urbina's old ranch. It was a property or two over—a little hacienda Urbina had built for his mistress. The gold and silver was at the bottom of a false well that Urbina had built to stash weapons for the revolution."

"So you found the treasure," I said. "But then you lost it. How?"

"Well, getting back to the lady's implicit point about subterfuge and betrayal, I took advantage of the fact that Jake was a city boy, a real tenderfoot. He relied on me as guide, cook. I cinched his saddles so he didn't fall off and break his neck; I saw to his horse's feeding and care. Jake was along as muscle and an extra gun. He was a good shot, though I never saw him fire under the stress of mortal combat. Those *federales* that killed our guards? We ran from them. Hard to know how he'd have shot with bullets flying back at him. But you know how that is."

"Sure." You never wanted to learn in the field—though Bud, back-shooting aside, acquitted himself well enough. "You got him lost out there in the desert," I said. "So he wouldn't really know where the treasure was."

"That's right," Emil said. "But then, even Jake started to pick up some familiar landmarks out there as I led him in circles. He started to catch on. Jake correctly accused me of trying to get him lost and confused. Thing was, I wasn't as sharp about doing it as I'd hoped to be. Wasn't thinking too clearly. Then I realized I was getting ill. We found the gold and silver; gathered it. And then I realized I was deathly ill. Really thought I might die. I'd come down with amoebic dysentery. I won't go into great detail, on account of we're eating and the lady's here."

Alicia shook her head. "I've had some nurse's training. I know about it."

A few years before our split, Hemingway had come down with the same thing in Africa. It plagued him for months. I said, "A former friend of mine had a case of that. Nasty stuff."

Emil grimaced and shook his head. "I began to hallucinate, to talk … and Jake exploited that cursed loose tongue of mine. He drew me out and soon knew I meant to lose him out there in the desert—to eventually abandon him or kill him. Bad position he was in. And me too. Real 'Mexican standoff.' But Jake was alone out there with me and all that treasure. He didn't stand a chance of finding his way back home alone. And he spoke little Spanish. If he did find his way to a town, he'd be robbed and killed by some Mexican. He knew that.

"We managed our way back to Urbina's mistress' house. Jake, he started nursing me. While I slept, Jake, he took that gold and that silver, pieces at a time, and he rode up into the hills somewhere, or something—hid it all. Maybe put it in an *arroyo* or something. Whatever the case, he'd later tell me it was very confusing and involved at least ten landmarks and some very specific numbers of paces between each marker. I didn't have a chance of finding the treasure on my own, he swore. And I believed Jake. So he was in a position to dictate terms. He said he'd get me through the stomach thing, and in return I had to get him back to civilization—get him to some place civilized and crowded, where my hand would be staid. Then we would come to terms about recovering the treasure. I'd get him back to that little mysterious ranch, and he would go out there in the desert and lead me to the place he'd hidden it. Well, lead *us*, 'cause I figured we'd each go back to Durango with our mutual mercenaries. We'd proven we couldn't trust one another, and I'd already made it clear I'd go to mortal lengths to screw him."

Alicia couldn't help herself. She said, "And here we sit, getting ready to negotiate with you."

"We're in Los Angeles," Emil said to Alicia, as if that abrogated decades of duplicity.

"But the treasure is still down there in my country," she persisted. "And we have to trust you to recover it and give us a cut."

"Don't sweat that," I said. "That's my territory. There'll be no double-crosses along those lines on my watch." I turned back to Holmdahl. "So, apparently, Jake Chrisman pulled you through and you both got back up to the border."

"Close to it," Emil said. "Very close. But it was getting dicey. The strain and the distrust started to accumulate on Jake. He started bleeding rectally—ulcers. Started drinking heavily. We both became afraid he might forget the map he had in his head. I was afraid he might die before he shared his secret. But he couldn't quite bring himself to write it down. He knew once it was out of his head, I'd redouble my efforts to get that treasure for myself. He just knew me too well."

Fiske nodded and closed his Zippo, blowing smoke through his nostrils from another Pall Mall. "So what happened? How'd we get to the point that we're sitting here negotiating for a severed head?"

"That's exactly what happened," Holmdahl said. "That fucking head of Pancho Villa's. That's where I finally lost the treasure. Or so I thought."

31

"I needed cash," Holmdahl said. "As I often did in those days. I was still weak and half out of my head from the sickness. Some old associates caught up with me across the border from El Paso as Jake and me were dancing around our dilemma. I was offered twenty-five grand to go in and cut off Pancho's head. You know that part of the story—or at least you know it close enough to the probable truth of the events. So we'll gloss that. Suffice it to say that I stole the fucking head—me and another old crony, Alberto Corral. I tried to talk Jake into doing it with me. But he refused. He tagged along though … I'd insisted he stay close. And he needed me alive to provide that starting point in order for his goddamn map to make any sense.

"Me and Alberto got the head," Holmdahl said. "But the resulting heat on us was terrible. Biblical. Seems I'd been graceless doing my recon before we dug up Pancho and hacked off his head. Again, I chalk it up to my sickness. My brain was soup. Anyhow, it quickly became clear to me that I was the prime suspect in the theft of Pancho Villa's head. So, in a kind of epic desperation, I entrusted

Jake with the bandit's head. Jake knew most of my plan. He knew I was to hit an airfield that night and pass the head off to a pilot and get my money. Well, then I got arrested for robbing Villa's grave. I was put in jail and told I'd be shot by a firing squad for stealing Villa's head."

"But Jake Chrisman really had the head," Alicia said.

"That's right," Emil said. "Jake bought himself some magician's flash paper in a novelty store. That paper explodes when it's exposed to any kind of heat. Then he bought himself some books on codes and invisible ink and the like. Jake came up with the gimmick of using ammonia and red cabbage water. He then emptied his head of his remembered map. Got it all down on that fragile magician's paper and hid it in Pancho's head. Then he went out to the airport and handed over the head and got my twenty-five grand, the cocksucker."

Bud smiled at me. I said aloud the words I knew we were all thinking. "Honor among thieves. *Yeah.*"

"Yeah," Emil agreed. "What a crock. But I was in a fix, make no mistake about it. Jake said he was my attorney and visited me in the Parral jail. Said he'd act as an intermediary and get word back to some people in high places in El Paso about my plight. They had helped set up the deal with Pancho's head and they had ties to Skull and Bones. They couldn't afford the embarrassment of me potentially finger-pointing at them to the press. But Jake, he'd only do this if I gave him the location of the farm where we'd found the treasure. He had me by the short hairs and we both knew it. He was so confident of his plan, he told me about the clever little map he'd hidden in Pancho's head. He smiled smugly and said he figured he'd remember the directions, and if he didn't, he could always go to Yale and steal the map back. But either way, he meant to have the treasure before I got out."

"So you lied to him," I guessed. "Gave him a false starting point."

"Fuck yes," Emil said, grinning. "I lied through my teeth. And the dumb cocksucker believed it. I could tell. Me? I know when I'm being lied to. Like I warned you."

Emil was getting passionate now. He'd apparently forgotten all about Alicia and her delicate sensibilities, just spewing that profanity now.

"Way I figured it, when I got sprung, I'd go to Yale and steal that fucking head a second time. Then I'd go down to Urbina's whore's ranch and take that treasure for myself while Jake and his crew dug dry holes in Dogdick, Durango."

Bud asked, "So what went wrong?"

"Well, I knew something went south on me when Prescott Bush called me up at the jail; well, one of Prescott's flunkies called, to be strictly accurate. He wanted to know why I'd 'screwed Bush.' Why I had 'taken' the Bush money and not 'supplied' the head. Well, it became clear to me that the pilot who'd taken the head from Jake Chrisman had cut his own deal with some previously unknown and scheming cocksucker. Never really knew who the mystery man was, or where Villa's head finally ended up, but suffice it to say that Pancho's skull never got to Yale. Some say the pilot was bought off by Brigadier General Francisco R. Durango, who drilled holes in the skull to use it as a caddy for his fountain pens. Others say it was Alvaro Obregón. Some say it was sold to a medical institution in Cleveland to some quack sawbones obsessed with severed heads. Either way, the skull was lost, and the treasure map with it."

Alicia sipped some iced tea. She said, "But Jake Chrisman knew the path to the gold, presumably."

"Right," Holmdahl said. "Presumably he did. But like I said, you gotta know where to start. He was provisioning in El Paso, I

heard, for a 'prospecting' job. He was going to go to that bogus lo-
cale I'd given him. But as Jake left the hardware store, probably dis-
tracted by dreams of all the treasures he envisioned having to himself, he was run over by a beer truck. The driver's side tire flattened
Jake's head—squeezed his brains and all those precious memories
out his ears. And, so, poor, put-upon and long-suffering Emil was
fucked up the ass by the fates … *again*."

"Sometimes luck runs that way," I said, rolling my eyes. "Well,
now we're all up to speed and know the lay of the land. And we've
pretty firmly established you're not to be trusted, Emil, and, well,
let's be frank—I just can't be trusted, either. We're both just old and
greedy campaigners who mean to dick one another."

Emil smiled. "About how I read it, too. So what do you
suggest?"

I tapped the table with my fingers. "I suggest you buy me out
right now. Well, me and my two young associates. I can't trust
you to go and get that gold and give me an honest cut. The young
lady here has already pointed that sad fact out. And, you know,
I have no interest whatsoever in going down to hell and living
that *Treasure of the Sierra Madre* motif you alluded to earlier. I'm
too old and happy in my air conditioning. I ain't gonna bust my
hump over a shovel in Durango … all the while waiting for you
to put a bullet behind my ear. Fuck that. You give me a hundred
grand—'cause I'm cheap—and we give you your map and we all
walk away happy."

The mercenary snorted. "Where in fuck would I get a hundred
grand?"

"Get it from some of your real estate cronies … from Texas
Republicans. Maybe you can sell a replica Villa head back to the
Mexican government for some recovery fee. That's not my problem.
I want to do this tomorrow. Get it over with. Your homework is to
find that money. And don't use the next few hours to try and fuck-

over me and mine by stealing the head or sending hired guns after us to take it. The head is in a safety deposit box. I have one key. An hour before we sat down to eat here with you, I dropped the key in a mailbox. I mailed it to someone somewhere here in Los Angeles, who'll have it delivered somewhere special in time for our exchange."

"I can't get that kind of money," Emil said.

"Don't insult me. I'm convinced you can. It's your problem to solve, either way."

The old soldier of fortune licked his lips. He said, floating a compromise, "Maybe half that I could do."

"Negotiations were never opened. One hundred grand." I handed Emil a slip of paper. "You call there with questions or comments. It's my answering service. Failing word to the contrary from you, before ten in the morning tomorrow, you're going to contact the bank on the flip side of that piece of paper and you're going to make a deposit. The account information you'll need is all there. You'll do this by ten a.m. At ten-thirty tomorrow morning, I'll call and confirm the deposit has been made. When I know it has, I'll meet you in front of Grauman's Chinese Theatre. High noon. I'll give you what's in the head there and then we're quits for keeps."

The mercenary shook his head. "Unacceptable. The risk is all on my end. You might take my money and run."

"Might. But it's the deal I'm offering. Simple."

"I don't think we're through figuring this one out," Emil Holmdahl said.

"I do."

"I'll think about it," the old man said bitterly.

"Sure. You do that, if it helps you feel better about yourself. But it makes no difference in the end. We're going to do this my way. That's it."

I settled the bill. Alicia unnecessarily wanted to touch up her lip-stick. Bud had gone to take a piss, or maybe shoot up some insulin.

Alone with Holmdahl, I said, "While back, Bud asked a question you never answered, Emil. How'd you avoid getting yourself killed by Fierro all these years?"

"We had a run-in a time back—pretty ugly. But we reached a kind of stalemate."

"What? Made a 'separate peace'?" I couldn't quite buy that.

"No," Emil said. "More like mutually assured destruction. I don't fear that cocksucker."

Emil and me walked out front. It was raining and we stood under the awning, looking out at the palm tree-lined streets of Los Angeles in the softly falling rain. "I never thought I'd end up here," Holmdahl said.

I nodded as I lit my cigarette. "I was surprised to find you here. Figured you'd be in some border town around El Paso, one side of the river or the other."

"Ain't much of any account left anywhere, you know? Used to be a man could make his way in this world ... make his money and live a good life doing it. But now? The world's gone to hell. Apart from this thing we're partnering on, well, I'm reduced to doing real estate finagling. What the fuck is that?"

"I hear you."

Emil spat. "It's a bitch to outlive your world, ain't it?"

"It surely is."

Emil looked at me and then gave me a nasty smirk as he gestured at my cigarette. "Well, at least I've had the good sense to take care of my-self. I won't end up old *and* a cripple." The "like you will" was implied.

Christ, but the old bastard knew how to go for the jugular.

"*Mañana*," I said, as I headed to my Chevy to wait for my young friends.

32

HOLMDAHL climbed into a cab. Through the rain-smeared windshield of my Chevrolet, I watched him leave.

Across the street sat another blue Chevy. There was an old Mexican in a Stetson behind the wheel. I got this strange feeling … muttered to myself, "Fucking Fierro." I climbed out and locked my Chevy and trotted through the now-harder rain, back to the Aero Squadron. Alicia and Bud met me at the door. My lady squeezed my arm. "That man—Holmdahl—he is not to be trusted," Alicia said. "He's truly evil."

"Yeah," I said. "Go to the bar, Alic. We all need to kill a few moments."

Bud's eyes narrowed. "What's up?"

"There's an old Mexican running surveillance from a car out front."

"Fierro, you think," Alicia said.

"*Sí.* I think. Go get yourself a drink, honey. We'll join you in a moment." I turned to Bud. "You're with me, poet. While I call the cops, you check the yellow pages for a magic supply shop."

"Flash paper?" Bud said.

"Flash paper," I confirmed.

As Fiske thumbed through the yellow pages, I called the cops. Breathless and strident, I told them I saw "some old Mexican pervert" sitting in his car, masturbating and trying to entice children into his Chevy. I gave the location and hung up.

We collected Alicia. When the squad car pulled up behind Fierro, the three of us walked to my Chevy and drove away.

Of course I figured that we had other tails.

Maybe frat boys.

Certainly federal agents.

The good, the corrupt … and Christ only knew what other kinds.

* * *

There was a bookstore next to Gibson Walter's Magic Shop. Alicia and me roamed the bookshop while Bud bought that flammable novelty paper.

As she browsed in the fiction section, I picked up a final edition of the day's *L.A. Times* and leafed through it. There was a small but shrill late-breaking item in the rag regarding a mysterious and brutal attack against the newspaper's book reviewer. The police blotter item indicated that the reviewer, Lee G. Todd, might permanently lose the use of his right hand. I felt a slight thrill, but I also felt slightly sick inside.

I studiously folded up the paper, replaced it and joined Alicia.

The store stocked seven or eight of my novels. There seemed to me to be a few too many copies on the shelf of *The Land of Dread and Fear*, my newest novel. Only one or two copies of each of my other titles were stocked. But there were perhaps nine copies of my new novel. *Hmm.* I felt a little less guilty about Lee G. Todd, suddenly.

"Which should I read?" Alicia fanned paperback copies of four of my novels that she apparently hadn't got to yet. I selected my Florida crime novel, *Last Key*. It is my most autobiographical. She smiled and nodded. While she paid, I checked a table up front where the bestsellers were laid out. I thumbed through a few, here and there: *Peyton Place* by Grace Metalious Messner; *Compulsion* by Meyer Levin; *Rally Round The Flag Boys* by Max Shulman; Nevil Shute's *On the Beach* and this fucking phone book-thick mess by Ayn Rand, dubbed *Atlas Shrugged*. (Probably did so because he couldn't support the weight of this undisciplined and self-indulgent mess of words.)

Sweet Jesus.

We walked back outside and waited under the awning in the drizzle for Fiske.

"Your grandmother is in town," I said to Alicia. "This could be a good time to visit your little girl. I'd love to meet her."

She shook her head. "No, Héctor. It is too risky. Too many people are maybe watching us now. Our danger is probably greatest about now, don't you think? I don't want to put my baby or anyone else I love at risk. And it would also be cruel to visit her, and then to leave right away again. I can't do that to either of us. I'll wait until this business is over. It's only one more day, yes?"

There was something more, I could tell. So I blundered ahead and said it. "You're also not sure you want her to know me. Not yet anyway. Yes?"

Alicia searched my eyes. She said, "Yes. That's right. I'm not sure yet."

33

THE rain was picking up when we got back to our rental.

I searched our "home," then let Alicia come in after I found nobody lurking in closets or under the beds.

We unloaded the real Pancho head and the good fake head with the underbite that we would foist on Emil Holmdahl. We also pulled out two of the backup heads.

We'd prep them, too, just in case.

We took out the little slip of paper we'd cut to match the original map and used it as a template to cut down the magic store flash paper to the right dimensions. Alicia searched the backyard and found a crow's feather we could use as a quill. I sat Bud down at the table and we concocted a Byzantine set of instructions involving trees that credibly might have been cut down or fallen over in the intervening twenty years, creek beds that might have run dry, boulders and swales. With any luck, the greedy bastards following the instructions would waste years of their lives in fruitless pursuit. Leave us all the hell alone.

The tough part for Bud seemed to be getting started. So I said, "There had to be a front door at the place Urbina built for his whore. Instruct them to walk one hundred paces straight out from the front step." We built our false map from that starting point.

Then I directed Bud to fill three more identical slips of paper with similar though slightly varying directions.

I privately relished the image of that bent federal agent and Holmdahl and maybe Fierro or Prescott Bush's lackeys all suddenly bumping into one another somewhere in the wastelands of Durango, all of them clutching identical slips of flash paper and counting their wasted footsteps.

Bud started to complain about writer's cramp. I shook my head and said, "At least you're not writing in your own piss. Soldier on, son."

"Yeah, about that," Bud said. "I just can't stand the thought of all that treasure lost out there at that ranch. Think there's any chance at all we could find it sans the real map?"

"None. Don't torture yourself, friend. It'd be impossible. And for all anyone knows, some Mexican bandits or peasants may have found it long ago."

We finished rigging the maps to the skulls. We did a good and credible job. It looked close enough to the same strange bump I'd found on Villa's real skull—just before I had stupidly torched that real fucking treasure map.

Afterward, I made a phone call. Eighty thousand American dollars had been deposited in my offshore account. That would be Prescott Bush's deposit for Pancho's head. I spent a few additional moments on the phone and had the funds transferred to yet another Swiss account. Soon, Alicia and her grandmother would begin receiving their too-lavish monthly support checks.

If Holmdahl kicked in his hundred grand, I'd pocket ten for expenses and split the rest between Bud and Alicia.

Alicia was in the bedroom, reading my Key West novel. I packed up Pancho's real head and drove to the post office. I boxed up the carpetbag nice and safe and covered it with lots and lots of tape. Then I mailed the bandit's head to myself, care of the hardware store in La Mesilla.

If I didn't die in the next twenty-four hours, I'd catch the head at the other end.

I had special, sentimental plans for that rotting skull.

When I returned, Bud was sitting out on the back porch, drinking a beer and scrawling away in a notebook. I said, "Sorry," and moved to leave.

"No, it's okay," he said. "It's not the real stuff. I'm just playing around with notes about you—for the article about you for *True*."

"Well then, that I *will* interrupt," I said. I'd grabbed my own beer. What could just one hurt?

We propped up our feet and watched the rain patter down as we sipped our Tecate.

Bud said, "What do you see yourself doing after all this?"

"I get the feeling what I want isn't in the cards," I said.

"Maybe," Bud admitted. "Maybe not right away, anyway. But if you get this behind you, get your health straightened out and stay away from the hooch and the blood, just do your work and be a square-john ... well, she might come around. It could really happen for you, you know."

I smiled and bit my lip. "What odds would you really give me on that?"

Bud thought a moment, then said, "Sober and staid? I think sixty-forty."

"No shit?"

"I may be an optimist," he said.

"Yeah, just like me." It was quiet a while, then I said, "You ever hear of the Tarahumara Indians, Bud?"

"No, sir."

"They call themselves the *Rarámuri*. They live in the Sierras, in and around Copper Canyon. The Spanish chased them up into the Sierras ages ago. What they mostly do is run—all day and all night. A few have entered races north of the border. They nearly always win—even running, as they do, in sandals made of rope and discarded tire treads. The Indians themselves don't really even call what they do 'running.' They call it 'foot throwing.' They have a game they play with a wooden ball called *Rarjíparo*. I reckon it's a little like soccer. But these games go on for days at a time. One day, I'd like to maybe take a train and see them; watch 'em play that game. Try and figure out how they can run so hard for so long."

There was thunder now, lightning.

"I'll leave you to your article." I was proud of myself—I was walking away from a half-a-bottle of beer.

Bud was starting to light up another cigarette. I said, "You should quit, before you really get hooked. Especially with your sugar problems."

"Probably."

"Really. I'm thinking of quitting myself. I've got morning phlegm issues you don't want for yourself. And lung cancer? I've seen three friends go that way. That fucking disease is why God invented guns and hard palates."

"I'll think about it," Bud said.

"That Zippo lighter you bought yourself … that inscription from my book … you being ironic, Bud, or what exactly?"

"Just a reminder and warning. I don't ever want to whore."

Hell, me either.

"I'll see you later," I said.

"Where are you going?"

"I'm going to go pick up my new eyeglasses," I said.

I did that. I hated them. But damn—now I could remember what it was like to really see. And Holy Christ—things looked even worse than I remembered.

Then I went to a tavern and borrowed a phone. I shared the rough outlines of my plan for the day with Agent Brown. I secured a promise that in exchange for helping Brown to "nail" his "partner" for J. Edgar, the fed would do what he could to keep the IRS off my back. I think in time he came to believe what was the gospel truth—that I wouldn't be keeping all that blood money coming my way in the morning.

Agent Brown also confirmed that Fierro had been questioned and released after I fingered him for being some kid-raping monster.

Seemed the old man was now going under the name of "Jesús Martínez."

He was under surveillance, Brown said.

Emil Holmdahl was under surveillance.

My new house was under surveillance.

So I said, "Anyone watching Prescott Bush?"

I could hear the rueful smile in Brown's voice. "Sure. Sure." Then, "One more thing, Hector. Mark that skull you give Holmdahl in some way, would you? So we can know if somebody tries to swap heads later, yes?" We agreed I'd scratch an "x" in the right, remaining, rear-most molar.

He paused, then said, "It's a shame, but I don't think you're going to get yourself a novel out of this one, partner."

"Not and not get indicted," I agreed.

34

I returned to the wonderful little tavern I'd found near our new place.

Some of my luck was running good. Buddy Loy Burke, my new favorite singer/songwriter, was back up there again, doing a wrenching version of "Canción Mixteca"—surely one of the most moving ballads of homesickness ever written. That guitarist by his side was just as brilliant as he had been the previous night.

For two hours I listened and applauded and expanded on my story about Alicia. I knew now it would be my next novel. Perhaps my last really good one. I was tying it all around the head of a famous Mexican bandit.

Three hours in, I again felt this hand brush across the back of my neck. Her timing, again, was perfect—I'd nearly emptied the well. I closed my notebook and stuck the pen in my sports jacket.

She was holding a Tequila Sunrise she had ordered for herself. I ordered a double shot of tequila, a tall glass of water and some fish tacos to split with her. She gestured at the stage. "That song, 'Canción Mixteca,' it's my favorite. He does it wonderfully, and with such soul. My grandmother used to sing me to sleep with that song."

"I think it's my favorite, too, now. I love it."

Buddy Burke and his partner ended their set and took a break. Alicia sang to me the lyrics of "our" song:

¡Qué lejos estoy del suelo donde he nacido!
inmensa nostalgia invade mi pensamiento
y al verme tan solo y triste cual hoja al viento
quisiera llorar, quisiera morir
de sentimiento.

¡Oh tierra del sol,
suspiro por verte!
ahora que lejos
yo vivo sin luz, sin amor

y al verme tan solo y triste cual hoja al viento
quisiera llorar, quisiera morir
de sentimiento.

She finished and smiled and shrugged.

"You could make a living doing that," I said.

"Only for undiscerning gringos like you," she said, chucking under my chin. Alicia was already slightly drunk. That bothered me, somehow.

"Your Key West book, you bastard," she said, "it broke my fucking heart."

I frowned. "You don't talk like that. You don't use those words."

"You do. Your women, in your books, often do."

"But *you* don't," I said. "Don't start now."

"Maybe it's time I did."

I pushed her drink away from her. "No, it isn't."

"You're going to try and die on me tomorrow, Héctor. I can tell. All your men die."

"You're wrong. I don't want to die. I have no choice about getting old; but I do about dying. This isn't one of my books. I still have … a few plans."

She looked up at me from under long black lashes. "I know that you do. We both know you do. But talking about your plans is the surest way to hear God laugh."

Alicia looked at her drink. She looked at the empty stage. She squeezed my hand. "Bud has found his own bar. He's writing poetry there. He said not to wait up for him. So let's go home. I know it bothers you, but tonight, I feel like feeling like one of those women you've written so much about."

35

ALICIA was twitching in her sleep … lost in the throes of some semi-gentle nightmare, I reckoned.

I shook her just enough to shift the patterns of her dreams, then I pulled the sheet up around her and slipped from our bed, showered and shaved and started coffee.

This morning, this one time, I vowed not to write anything.

Bud had been up for hours—already showered and shaved and revising his early morning's work.

As Alicia bathed, I called my Swiss bank. The hundred-thousand dollars had been deposited by Emil Holmdahl or his associates. Probably the latter. Part of me suspected that Emil had his own car trunk filled with heads. Soon the blackest of black markets would be flooded with Pancho Villa skulls. Either way, it worked for me, or more precisely, for *mine*—the cash was safely in hand. I again transferred the funds, then closed out the account into which Prescott Bush and Emil Holmdahl had made their deposits.

I loaded my Peacemaker. I also had a derringer in the cuff of my right boot. That last wouldn't do much, but you never know when even a dainty holdout might give you an edge.

Bud had his inherited .45 tucked down in his waistband at his back. He was learning.

Alicia was not feeling well. Probably her first bad hangover—a result of my exerting more bad influence. She also complained of a sore throat. I suggested she stay home. She resisted and it was just as well—I wanted her in sight, where I could look after her. As a "compromise," she brewed a thermos of chamomile tea. Bud ran to the corner to buy her a little bottle shaped like a bear and filled with honey that she could take along to mix with the tea.

While they finished packing, I told them we'd likely not be in position to return to this place; told them just in case to pack everything they couldn't bear to abandon. Then I went into the garage and I opened the trunk of my Chevy and went about preparing the arsenal that Bud and me had amassed over the past several days. Afterward, I arranged the heads in their respective bags in a very deliberate sequence.

Once all that was prepared, I walked to the corner liquor store and bought a silver flask and a bottle of single malt Scotch. I filled the flask and tossed the rest of the bottle. I tucked the flask into the cuff of my left boot, just in case.

We loaded into the car and we drove to Hollywood Boulevard. I palmed into a space in front of Grauman's Chinese Theatre.

Emil Holmdahl was already loitering there, his bony ass parked on the rear fender of his '56 Rambler station wagon. To all appearances, he was alone.

I climbed out, smiling. "I got your deposit," I said. "Thanks so much for that."

As I'd instructed, Alicia and Bud remained in my Bel Air. But Bud had one of the Tommy guns resting at his feet. I opened the trunk and pulled out the first carpet bag in the line. I quickly closed the trunk and moved around to the front of my car. I rested the bag on the hood of my Chevy and opened it. "Here it is," I said to Emil Holmdahl. "Your fucking map is in the right eye. But you know that." I offered him a pair of tweezers. He smiled and accepted them. Then he did what I had always expected him to do—the cocksucker pulled a gun on me. Two Mexicans had also stepped up, either side of my car. They had on long coats but each pulled those back to give us all glimpses of the sawed-off shotguns they were hiding under those conspicuous black dusters.

Then this other old Mexican came striding out of the theatre. He grinned at me like a moustachioed death's head.

"Hey, Fierro," I said, trying to steady my quaking knees. "How's tricks, *hombre*?"

He spat on my boot.

I said to Holmdahl, "You said you and Fierro had reached a Mexican standoff so to speak … looks more like a rapprochement. Hell, a partnership."

Emil smiled. "Like I told you, Lassiter, my enemy's enemy …"

I shook my head. "Jesus, the two of you working together—there really is nothing you won't do for money, is there, Emil?"

"Look at you, Lassiter," Emil said. "Trying to act tough and cool, like one of your characters. But you ain't fooling me. You look more dejected than a four-dollar whore on nickel night." Emil Holmdahl handed the old Mexican the bag with the head. The soldier of fortune said, "Little feller, he's got the big underbite. Looks real to me. What do you think?"

The Butcher grunted. "One can never be truly sure after so many years," he said. Try as I might, I couldn't *truly* read that old bastard Fierro's expression. I couldn't be certain that he'd bought our deception. "So much rot. But, yes, I concur." As he said this, he reached under my coat and took my Peacemaker. He smiled and held it up. "No," Emil said to him. "You can't keep it. That ain't cricket. That's his gun. You know how that is. Empty it and give it back to him."

Fierro sneered at the mercenary. "Fuck you, *gringo*. This gun looks worth much money."

Emil turned his gun on Fierro. "Some things aren't done, asshole. Never a man's horse, or his gun. Empty the bullets out and give him the Colt back."

Fierro opened my gun, spun the cylinder. He threw the bullets at Emil's feet. He shoved the gun down my waistband, the sight scraping my thigh. *Cocksucker.*

"So you're going to sell the skull to Bush after you take the map out," I said to Holmdahl. "I should have seen it coming." I looked back and forth between Fierro and Holmdahl. "But then, in the nearer term, I'd hate to be either one of you sons of bitches. Hard to say which of you is the bigger snake. I don't see this as a steady partnership. Don't envy either of you the next hour or two."

Both old men winked at me. My skin crawled.

One of the younger Mexicans reached into my Chevy and pulled my car keys from the ignition. He tossed them into traffic.

"*Vaya con Dios*, you sorry asshole," Emil said, backing toward his Rambler.

Fierro smiled and tipped his Stetson. He was backing toward the theatre.

Emil waved at the Butcher and said, "See you at the rendezvous."

When they and their buddies were gone, holding up a hand to stop traffic, I walked out and retrieved my car keys. Then I swung behind the wheel of my Chevy.

"Well, that all went to hell," Bud said.

"Did it?" I smiled. "We all knew Emil would try to screw us. But we have Prescott Bush's money. We have Emil's hundred grand. Emil and Rudy will try to dick one another, of course. Frankly, I'd hate to make book on who comes out ahead there. But really, it's academic. Because before those cocksuckers turn guns on one another, Agent Duane David is going to intercept Emil.

"Duane is a bent FBI agent," I continued. "A Yale grad. And a Skull and Bones member. He has his own designs on that treasure. And he sees himself currying favor with the Bush family, down the road. He'll give them the skull so Prescott will be appeased. But there's more. Agent David's partner, Kenneth Brown, is going to move on David for betraying the FBI, for secretly working for the CIA on American soil. That's one big no-no. And worse, he was betraying the agency and wicked J. Edgar. So Duane's just bought himself an Old Testament-style ass fucking. So, it all balances out in the end. Except maybe for Fierro. Him, I may have to track down later ... personally put him down."

Alicia squeezed some honey into the tea she had poured into the lid of her thermos. "Can it really all play like this? As you've plotted it?"

"Sure. It could. It should. Why the hell wouldn't it?"

36

WE returned to our Tom Mix bungalow a last time.

Bud borrowed my car and headed out to a tavern to write. I told him about my favorite new singer and L.A. tavern and he headed over there.

Alicia and I pulled the shades and went to bed. We were both sober and it was sad and slow this time. I could tell she was torn. Had me this sense that maybe young Bud was right—I might actually have a shot at finessing this lady into my life. Afterwards, hearts pounding against one another, I found her hand and squeezed. I said, "In the book, I get the girl."

She brushed the damp hair back from my forehead and said softly, "The men in your books never get the girl."

"I'm thinking about turning over a new leaf, so to speak."

"If that is so, then you would have to write very different books."

I nodded. "I know. But it's maybe getting to be that time of life."

She smiled and hugged me hard.

We showered together, then sat out on the back porch. At my request, she began to sing an *a cappella* version of "Canción Mixteca." She sang it like a torch song this time, in that smoky voice she had.

I heard three gunshots—fired out front.

"Get in the bedroom, my Colt is there," I said, rising. "I've reloaded it. Lie down under the bed. Anyone looks under the bed, you shoot the fucker in the face." Then, unarmed, I vaulted the back porch railing. That was slick—didn't know I still had such gymnastics in me. Pumped, I hurdled the chainlink fence that surrounded the bungalow's backyard. When I hit the ground, I wrenched my ankle—pain all the way up to my right knee.

Half-limping, half-running, I edged around to the front of our place. Two Mexicans were beating on Bud Fiske. Several cars were approaching. The Mexicans threw Bud into my Chevy and tore off. Behind my Bel Air was a second Chevy. Rodolfo Fierro was behind the wheel and another Mexican was with him. A third car, a Buick, pulled out behind that. Didn't get a look at those guys, but there seemed to be at least five in the car.

I screamed and pounded the wall of the bungalow.

Jesus Fucking Christ! Poor Bud, goddamn him, in the hands of that sadistic, bloodthirsty motherfucker. *Jesus.*

Then I heard a single shot and watched as the back window of Fierro's Chevy exploded. Alicia had ignored my warning—retrieved my gun and put a bullet through the back of the car. I doubted she hit anyone, but maybe she'd at least give the old cocksucker a heart attack—stroke him out before he could hurt poor Bud.

Neighbors were peering through their windows, mouths open.

Let in one pulp writer and there goes the neighborhood.

I limped around the corner. Alicia was wild-eyed, waving my Colt. "We'll stop someone driving by, take their car and chase them," she said, breathless.

"No. They have us outgunned. And they have too big a headstart."

Alicia's eyes implored me. "I'll call the police," she said, "report your car stolen."

"No, it would take too much time. By the time we got those cops on our side, Bud ..." I didn't have to finish that.

Carefully, I pulled my Colt from her hands. "Try to flag down a taxi while I make a phone call."

"Not the police?"

"No, someone better."

He was deep into paperwork spinning out from the detention of his "partner," so it took a full five minutes for him to answer. I laid out the situation for Agent Kenneth Brown and said, "You can still track my car electronically, yeah?"

"Yeah, I can. But I think the agency's interest in this matter—"

"Stop," I said. "Don't even say it. I know where too many bodies are buried. I'm a writer with a lot of connections. It would be bad for all of us if I turned whistle-blower. Move now and you can maybe be back in time for dinner, with time to spare to continue putting it to Agent Duane David."

I could tell he'd cupped a palm around the receiver. Then Agent Brown said, "Okay. The Director has agreed." Jesus—J. Edgar was personally there? He must really have a hard-on for Duane. "Get a cab or something and get yourself over to MacArthur Park," Brown told me. "Do it now."

"Why there?"

"Because we can land a helicopter there."

37

WE had to shout over the chop of the blades above us. I'd tried to talk Alicia into staying, or into accepting Agent Brown's offer of an armed escort to a safe place until we had recovered Bud—or what was left of him—but she refused.

It had been several hours since Bud was snatched. For too long, we had been chasing the faint echoes of the signal from my car. But only echoes; no firm fix.

Agent Brown had explained the limitations of the tracking device. Essentially, we could stay within a ten mile range of the transmitter in my car and still read a signal, but there would be no variability in signal strength in populated areas—nothing to indicate we were getting hotter or colder "in terms of acquiring a sight target." There would be too much interference from other signal sources in greater Los Angeles—problems caused by radio and television signals, HAM radio operators and the possibility of other FBI tracking devices being employed in the area that could send us off target. "I mean, it's Los Angeles for Christ's sake," Brown said, "… so many goddamn communists working in Hollywood …"

I shook my head. "Really? That's still true? What was HUAC for?"

"I'll ignore that," Brown said. "Only place worse than greater Los Angeles to try and follow somebody would be New York City. But we can be sure they are headed south. When they get out a ways from the major cities, it will be easier to zero in on them, eyeball them. And if he gets into the boonies, then we can land this son of a bitch on the roof of your Bel Air, I think. We've got a handheld tracker, if we get close enough, that will give us signal strength, but we'll really have to be in the sticks to use that."

Now we were hovering over San Diego, and our fix was no firmer.

For now, the only hopeful thing was that there was still an indication of movement—that motion would make it harder to be too inventive in terms of torturing my poor young poet. But we had no line of sight on my fleeing Chevy—no hard target.

And if Bud had been moved from my Chevy to another vehicle? Well, the likely results were too terrible and tragic to contemplate. Didn't stop me from trying, of course.

As we'd flown south, we'd gotten a bit of a fill on the aftermath of the head exchange.

Holmdahl had somehow succeeded in switching heads on Agent Duane David. That seemed to surprise to Agent Brown. But not me—it was impossible to overestimate Emil. The switch had been confirmed because the head David had when he was captured had no "x" carved into its right rear molar. Although it *did* boast its own hidden map written on flash paper.

Crafty Emil.

And he walked away clean—nothing really on Holmdahl that could be used.

Their respective tails had reported no rendezvous between Emil and Fierro. I could only assume Fierro hadn't been convinced by the phony skull that I'd allowed Emil to steal. It would explain why Fierro came looking for me and mine to try and recover the real head and accompanying treasure map.

Brown said, "What kind of firepower do you think they have?"

I swallowed hard, thinking. I really didn't want to go into trying to explain the arsenal in the trunk of my Bel Air that they might have found by now. "Can't say for sure," I said. "At the head exchange on Hollywood Boulevard, there were a couple of sawed-offs, some handguns. But a while back, they actually fired a couple of Thompsons at me."

"And you're still standing?" Brown's eyebrows arched. "You're better than you look. Or they're inept."

"Let's hope both are true."

The pilot signaled to Brown and he moved forward in a crouch to the cockpit to consult.

I reached into my boot cuff for the flask. I was unscrewing the lid when Alicia snatched it from me. She poured the contents on the floor. "How dare you?"

A shrug. "I'm trying to steady my nerves."

"And dull your reflexes … slow your mind," she said.

I sighed. "You're right, of course. Use the adrenaline." *Right.*

"We have a problem," a voice said behind me. I turned. Brown leaned in close to my ear. "We're getting a better fix now. Thing is, they may now be outside my reach."

The fucking border. They'd crossed into Mexico and right outside FBI jurisdiction.

"Christ, I knew I should have thrown in with Duane," I said. "At least the CIA is extra-territorial. You're of no fucking use to me now."

Agent Brown got his finger up in my face. "Hey, fuck you! I'm amazed we've come this far together. I'm frankly shocked you've been given this level of agency support and access to resources by the Director. So fuck you, Lassiter."

I could feel the heat of Alicia's angry gaze on me. I needed to tamp down my anger—try and play ball for Bud's sake. "I'm sorry, Brown," I said. "I know you can't risk it—doing something in Mexico that could make news. All I have on me now is an antique Colt. Give me a little more firepower and take me in as close as you can, please? Enough for a short walk, but not so close they'll hear this fucker coming in at them."

Brown thought this through. "I should consult with Mr. Hoover. But—in a circumstance like this—well, maybe it's better to ask forgiveness than permission." He looked at Alicia and then back at me. "How many do you think there are?"

"At least four." I thought of that third car. "But maybe eight or nine."

"Nine on one?" Brown said. "I sure don't like your odds."

"Me either."

Alicia shook her head. "Nine on two."

I grabbed her arms and squeezed. "Oh, fuck that! For Christ's sake—you've got a little girl. And you've never really fired a gun."

She shook her head. "But Bud …"

Brown was shaking his head, too. "This was all a mistake."

"Then send for help," Alicia said, pleading.

"Wouldn't reach us in time," I said.

"Wouldn't matter, either way," Brown said. "That pilot up there would have to give coordinates—in fucking Mexico. There'd be no help granted and we'd be ordered back. And I've got kids, too … a mortgage. I'm too many years in the bureau to fuck up my pension now—or to start a second career."

"So we're back to my original proposition," I said. "Give me some good guns, then drop me close by them. I'll go in alone and I'll bring back Bud."

Agent Brown didn't like it. Alicia didn't like it. Hell, I didn't like it; not because of me, but because of poor Bud. It was a suicide run—like that hopeless fucking task Emil Holmdahl had described of trying to assassinate Villa in his homeland and then living to tell the tale later.

"They've stopped," the pilot said.

"Where?" Agent Brown and I asked simultaneously.

"Somewhere near Tijuana. Not as remote as we'd want. It's going to be hard to know exactly where. And if we fly over to verify ..."

Grand.

We hovered around a bit—perhaps another twenty minutes, trying to get a firmer fix on the location of my Chevy. Twenty long minutes ... I doubted that Fierro had taken more than ten minutes to dissect Urbina with bullets so many years ago. But I'd wager good money those ten minutes were an eternity of agony for the Butcher's victim.

"This is as good as it gets, people," the chopper pilot said. We lofted down and he cut the engines. As the dust settled, I checked my Colt. Brown gave me a pair of .45s, clips and a sniper's rifle. "You need instruction on any of these?"

I took them with a shaking hand. I hoped nobody noticed. Not fear—blood sugar. Adrenaline and the fact that I couldn't remember my last meal ... well, it was bad news. My vision was blurring and I was thirsty as hell. Felt vaguely nauseous.

Brown handed me a knapsack and I shrugged it over my shoulder. I said, "What's this?"

"A canteen and grenades. I trust you know how to use those, too. The grenades I mean."

"You can trust." I smiled at Alicia. "Back in a jiff."

She shook her head. "I'm coming."

"No way."

"I'm coming," she said. "Alone, you don't stand a chance."

Brown shook his head. "Goddamn it!" He grabbed a rifle and two extra .45s. He handed a walkie-talkie to Alicia. He said, "I'm going to come. But strictly as an observer. Consultant, only. I think we're at least a mile, maybe two miles out from these cocksuckers. Alicia will come the first mile with us. Then we go on ahead. I'll carry another radio. These things tend to get screwy out here in desert, with the bandit radio stations and shortwaves and weather conditions. This way, we stay in touch with the chopper so we can get out, *muy pronto*, if needed."

I checked my watch. In theory, once we reached them, Fierro might already have had forty-five minutes with Bud. I thought, *no more words.* "Let's go," I said. My mind was heavy with images of all the atrocities I'd ever heard attributed to Fierro—sliced-off soles of feet, ant trails, crucifixion and disembowelment.

Jesus Christ. Poor, poor Bud.

Brown toted a little, hand-held version of the tracking device in the helicopter. The thing had a little dial for adjustments and a needle that tracked signal strength, kind of like a Geiger counter. But it was still inexact stuff.

We walked perhaps a mile when we began to hear voices. Seems we were closer to them than we ever would have guessed. We edged along a nearly dried-up *arroyo*, staying close to the crisped scrub that lined the banks. On the opposite bank, there was a small cabin. Four Mexicans were gathered around something, looking down and laughing. Pointing. Occasionally they would stoop down and then stand up again.

I pulled out the sniper's rifle and began fiddling—my focus was very poor now. Brown seemed to confuse my loss of vision with ineptitude. "Here," he said. "Gimme."

He fiddled, then said, "Okay, there's four of them. Three young fellows, and one old man. He let Alicia look through the scope.

"It's him," she said. "It's Fierro."

"Any sign of Bud?" My voice sounded strange to me. And I was dying of thirst. I pulled out the canteen and took a deep drink. It didn't touch my thirst.

I pulled on my new glasses and took the gun from Alicia. I could see a little better now, but I wouldn't want to pull the trigger on a target that really mattered. I scoped around, trying to see what they were all gathered around … what they were dipping over.

Still couldn't see well, but I soon saw enough.

Bud had been stripped to the waist and lashed to some flimsy wooden framework. He was spread-eagled, face down, over a massive maguey plant. It was reputed to be a favorite torture tactic of Fierro's. They say Emiliano Zapata invented it. To help the process along, the cocksuckers were incrementally piling stones on Bud's bony back, forcing him down on the spikes. Wouldn't surprise me if they had already dislocated both of his arms at the shoulders with the weight of those rocks. I couldn't tell how far those goddamned spikes had already drilled into Bud's gut, but I could see blood on the plant.

And now we could hear Bud's terrible screams.

I said, "Alicia, get down as close to the ground as possible."

Brown said, "Lassiter, what are you—"

One of the young Mexicans was about to drop another rock on Bud's back. I aimed for his head. There was a blast furnace wind cutting west to east across the scrub. I tried to compensate for that wind and its effects across perhaps one hundred-fifty yards of desert. I pulled the trigger.

Like I said, my vision was bad. And, like I said, I aimed for that bloodthirsty bastard's head. I saw him drop the rock—I prayed not upon Bud—and clutch at his neck as blood sprayed from his throat. I'd missed my target by nearly a foot. But I'd killed that son of a bitch.

The leaves and stalks above our heads were cut by the first sweep of one of Fierro's flunkey's machine guns. I sighted in on another of the younger Mexicans. I was going for the center of his torso—an easier target—and hit that bad bastard in the head.

Then my vision completely fogged. I got down close to the ground.

"Brilliant," Brown said. "You stupid cocksucker."

"There are only two left," I said. "Even odds."

"You said there might be nine. Maybe the rest are in that cabin."

"Or maybe I was wrong."

Brown inched up between volleys and sighted in on the last of the young Mexicans. He fired.

I smiled hopefully and said, "You hit the cocksucker?"

"He has a third eye," Brown said, trying to sound angry but not quite getting there. I could tell he was impressed with his own marksmanship. And he was exhilarated in that way we get with bullets flying. He was positioning to fire on Fierro when his head snapped back. He grabbed himself between his throat and shoulder, low down on the neck. Arterial blood sprayed across my new glasses.

I fired twice with my Colt at Fierro and saw him fall—or dive. My vision was too faulty to distinguish between the two.

Brown was trying to speak, but going into shock. Alicia pressed her hand to his neck wound.

After I wiped the blood from my glasses, I picked up the sniper rifle and scoped around.

Fierro was in a crouch behind Bud, now. I could just get a glimpse at the top of his head. I tried to sight in, but my vision kept fuzzing. The odds of me hitting Bud—and hitting him in the heart or the head at this angle instead of hitting Fierro— were too high, even for a reckless bastard like me. If I were to pull the trigger, I'd have to conclude that Bud was likely to end up a dead man.

I squeezed the bridge of my nose and rubbed my eyes and tried looking through that goddamn scope again. My vision was even worse.

Now I could only really see motion and light through the scope.

Alicia said, frenzied now, "Shoot him, Héctor! End it! We have to help Bud and get help for the Agent."

I shook my head. "I—I can't *see*. The diabetes ... I can't see enough to take the shot. I'll kill Bud if I do. I know I'll kill him."

Her hands were pressed tightly to Brown's neck wound. Her brown skin was slick with Brown's blood. Alicia said, "You want me to try and kill him? That's what you're going to say, isn't it?"

Truth was, that terrible notion hadn't even occurred to me. My plan was more direct—I would rush Fierro. Try to get close enough to point my Colt like a finger at his body and fire until I ran out of bullets. We would trade slugs until one or both of us died.

"Put your hands here," she said. "Press hard."

"Alicia," I said, "I can't have you doing this. Killing a man—even a man like that, and like this—it changes you."

"We don't have time," she said. "He doesn't have time," she said, nodding at the man whose blood covered her hands. "Bud doesn't have fucking *time,* now. And we have no other options. You've seen to that, Héctor. Now put your fucking hands here and help this man."

Cursing, I laid the sniper's rifle down and shifted positions with her. As she took her hands away, a small geyser of blood erupted from Agent Brown's neck. I pressed my hand to his wound as Alicia took my former position. She picked the gun up awkwardly, trying to get it up against her shoulder. Her posture was wrong; her grip was all wrong. But it would have to do. After she pulled that trigger, she'd have a bruise on that right shoulder. But that bruise would fade. The other effects of the shot …? I felt sick inside.

I saw her adjusting the gun, trying to sight in on Fierro.

Licking my parched lips, I said hoarsely, "Do you see him yet?"

"Yes." I heard this intake of breath from her mouth. "Oh God, poor Bud."

"Don't look at him, darling. Focus on Fierro. You see the crosshairs?"

"Yes."

Put them on the tip of Fierro's nose, if you can see it."

"I can."

"Put them there then." Adjusting for wind, distance—there was no time to talk her through these things. Aiming at his nose would likely put the bullet in his mouth or chin, or high up on the forehead, or through either eye. It would likely take him out, either way.

I said, "When you feel the gun is steady, and those hairs are steady on your mark, take a deep breath, and then pull the trigger. Don't flinch when you do it. The bullet will be on its way before you can react, so don't anticipate the sound, or the kick of the rifle before they happen. Just take a deep breath, check your target a last time, and squeeze the trigger with even pressure."

I waited for what seemed like five minutes.

Then I heard the crack. I heard her scream and watched her head drop.

38

I said, "Alicia. Honey? Did you hit him?"

She was shaking all over. She turned to look at me, pulling the long, black curtain of hair from her face with a shaking hand. "I'm pretty sure."

"Come over here," I said, nodding at Agent Brown. "Please. Take over."

She slid back over and pressed her hands to Agent Brown's wound.

I retrieved the walkie-talkie and raised the pilot. I said, "Agent Brown is down. The others are all dead. We need you here now, and you need to get a hospital prepared to receive him in San Diego. We're near a shack about 1.5 miles south of your present location. It's the only structure in sight."

I squeezed Alicia's arm. "Chopper will be here in a minute. I'm going to go get Bud."

On shaking legs, my vision blurred, I ran low through the mesquite to where Bud was staked out. I kept my Colt out, waiting to be fired on by Fierro or some confederate of his who might be hiding in the brush.

But no more shots came.

Fierro was sprawled on his back, blinking and unable to speak. Alicia had shot him in the neck. His arms and legs weren't moving. Fierro was paralyzed, and maybe shot through the vocal chords, to boot.

The Butcher was alive, but it would be a hell of a way to spend one's declining years.

I holstered my Colt and dug out my Swiss Army knife.

"Are you with me, Bud?"

His voice was hoarse. "Hector? Oh thank Christ, Hector!"

"Don't move, son. I'm gonna cut your arms and legs loose, then we're going to count three and I'm going to pull you off that goddamned plant."

First, I pulled the rocks from his back. I wrapped an arm around his skinny torso to support his weight as I cut loose the ropes from his ankles and wrists and from around his waist.

I said, "On three." Then, before counting "one," I jerked him backward onto my lap.

He screamed and blacked out on me. I checked his pulse—he hadn't checked out for keeps.

Most of Bud's wounds looked superficial. Two looked deep. I tore off my own necktie and tore it into fat strips. I rolled up two of these and thrust them in Bud's deepest belly wounds. They'd pulled off Bud's boots and burned the soles of his feet with cigarettes. They had apparently done the deed with Bud's own cigarettes, judging from the stubs and the brand of the empty cigarette pack on the ground. If that didn't make him quit smoking, nothing would.

I got him up on my shoulder and then, grateful for his skinny-assed frame, I carried Bud Fiske a hundred yards across that sweltering desert.

Visions of heart attacks or hemisphere-paralyzing strokes loomed. As I drew closer, I squinted against the sand kicked up as the helicopter descended.

Bud came to as the helicopter settled to the ground. He said, "The skull didn't fool Fierro. He said Obregón was the one who intercepted the head all those years ago. Fierro was looking for a particular hole at the top of the head where Obregón kept his fountain pen. That's how he knew the one we gave Emil was a fake."

I said, "Don't talk, Bud."

Nearly done in, I reached the helicopter that was now waiting. Agent Brown was already inside and stretched out. Alicia was taping thick pads to his neck.

She said, "Is Bud alive?"

"He'll make it," I said.

"And Fierro?"

Goddamn me anyways, sometimes. I wanted Fierro to myself. I didn't think about the effect my callous lie would have on her.

I should have said, "Fierro is still alive. You saved Bud." That would have been good.

Instead I said the words *I* would have wanted to hear under those circumstances. I said, "You're a good soldier. You killed that monster dead. Put him down like a pro."

The look in her eyes … my God. I fancy myself a writer and I couldn't describe what I saw. But I knew I hated it. I knew on my best day at the writing table, I could never hope to capture that ineffable look of self-loathing she wore. And I hated myself for putting it there.

The pilot said, "We're low on fuel, and now we'd be flying out with one more than we went in with. And these guys are on their backs, so there's not much room. Can you see to yourself until I can get help here, sir?"

"Think Hoover will really send help?" I smiled. "My car is here. I'll drive myself back. I hoisted the radio. Just leave your unit on, so when I'm in range, you can maybe tell me which hospital to go to."

He smiled and nodded. "Gotta go and I mean now."

Alicia said to me, "You'll be alright, with the blood sugar?"

"I'll find something to eat. I'll be fine. I'm sorry—"

"Not now," she said.

I stood squinting at the glare from the windscreen as the helicopter lifted away. I waved goodbye to Alicia with my Colt in my hand.

* * *

The keys to my Bel Air were in the car. I opened the glove compartment and found a stash of crackers and melting candy bars Bud had put there. I wolfed down two candy bars and then walked back to Fierro.

I tried to get him to speak, but he couldn't. His eyes implored me.

So I smiled at him. There was an anthill about four feet from where they had staked out Bud. Fierro was probably saving that torture technique for later. I went back to my Chevy. I found that little bottle of honey shaped like a bear that Alicia had been using to spike her tea. I poured a thin trail of honey from the anthill over to Fierro. I emptied the bottle across his eyes, which, when I had finished, were opened wide, sticky and begging.

I said, "Don't run off."

Then I went into the shack. Not much there. I pulled the bodies of Fierro's lieutenants inside, found some old papers and fuel oil and torched the place with the corpses inside. Less for J. Edgar to have to fret over.

Before I left, I stood over Fierro a last time. The ravenous ants were about a foot from finding the Butcher. I leaned in close to Fierro and said, "*Viva Villa.*"

* * *

Two miles north of the shack, I hit a roadblock. I recognized the car—a Buick. It was that third vehicle that had fallen in behind Fierro's car when Bud was snatched hours before. Five young guys with guns were crouched behind the car. They yelled, "We want the head."

More fucking frat boys.

Christ, but I was soul sick of them and their ilk. I got out, my hands up. I walked to the back of my Chevy and opened the trunk. All those guns that Bud and me had collected were there, resting there at the ready.

Could have had me my own private Alamo out there on the outskirts of TJ.

It would have been a good and a colorful death. But I had dimming dreams of life with this Mexican lady and her little girl.

Grunting, I pulled out one of the carpetbags with one of the lesser heads and flung the thing into the dust between us.

I pointed at the bag and yelled to them, "Take it. Stick it in your fucking trophy cabinet. And now forget you know me, yeah?"

* * *

I had a lot of time in the car alone driving back up to San Diego.

Can't say I enjoyed the company.

39

THEY said that Agent Brown would pull through.

Alicia had finally taken a cab back home to her daughter and grandmother. I said I'd call her in a few days to check on her. That's all it would be, "checking in." Alicia had made it clear that I wouldn't be getting to know that little girl of hers.

She hugged me hard and left without kissing me.

Bud Fiske, recuperating, had borrowed a typewriter and locked himself in an L.A. hotel room to bang out his overdue article about yours truly.

"I'm having trouble figuring out how to write it," he confessed.

"Screw that," I told him. "Just do it. Make it up. Have fun with it. Build a legend around me."

The poet shook his head. "I can't do that."

"You have to, Bud. The last few days we've lived … nothing there to be used. Just make it up. It's what I do, all the time."

Bud looked skeptical. "Sure."

"Yeah—*sure*," I said, firmer now. "I do it every morning, at least three hours a day, every day, whether it's shit or not. Only way to get anything done. Besides, you can't ever tell *True* the truth."

"Alright then," he said finally, after some more pushing.

With Alicia gone and Bud busy writing, I was left at ends—always a dangerous way for me to be.

So I bit my lip, held my nose, and drove to Venice to close out my lingering business with Orson Welles.

* * *

Here's a secret for you. Next time that you watch *Touch of Evil*, carefully study those vignettes with Orson and Marlene. If you've got a good eye on you, you'll notice something. After an establishing shot in their very first scene, they are never again in frame together. When Marlene says her lines to "Hank Quinlan," that's me she's talking to.

Orson delivered his lines to some Mexican extra that at least should have been Alicia. But I'd cost her that gig, too.

That's my hand you'll see in the film, drunkenly spreading those damned fortune-telling cards. And I was drunk … flying on mescal.

After filming, safe in Marlene's trailer that was laced with the smell of her cooking and us, together, I rolled off her.

I reached down for a towel and wiped my cum from her flat belly. She sighed and stretched and moved her thigh over my crotch and ran her fingers through my chest hair. It was sweltering in the trailer. I leaned over and kissed her small, salty left breast.

"Thank you for doing this for Orson," she said.

"You know that I didn't do it for him."

"Then you'll do one more thing for me. You'll call Papa, won't you?"

I sighed. My Teutonic chanteuse was indomitable. "I will. But not tonight and maybe not tomorrow."

She bit my shoulder and I winced and knotted my fingers in her tousled hair—it was dark with dye for her role as "Tanya." I kissed her, hard. Marlene said, "Promise me, Hector. And make it a real promise, yes?"

"I promise, Kraut. Cross my heart—"

She quickly pressed her stained fingers to my lips. "The luck," she said. "Don't send those kinds of thoughts out into the world. It's enough for me that you promise."

"I want to spend the night here," I said.

Though we hadn't discussed her, Marlene seemed to know about Alicia and me. Maybe she had been playing with those damned Tarot cards that had been given to her as a prop for her character—perhaps in the cards she saw my plight.

Marlene smiled a sad smile. "Tonight you can stay."

I tipped my head back on her arm, my scarred hand stroking her flat belly.

She was softly singing something.

"What is that tune?"

"It's an old Mexican song that Papa taught me," she said. "I sing it with the German lyrics. It's called 'Canción Mixteca.'"

I felt the hairs rise on the back of my neck.

40

THAT morning, I spent an hour going over my car, fender to bumper, inside and out—tearing off gizmos that had been planted on it.

I called the management company and told them they had a rental back on their hands—let someone else enjoy that Tom Mix vibe.

Bud offered to let me read his first draft of my profile in typescript. I demurred. "I'm gonna love it, I'm sure," I said. "Besides, I need something to look forward to."

Bud nodded, looking reluctant. "So what now?"

"I need to get back down to New Mexico. To pick up a parcel … make a delivery."

"What parcel?"

"Pancho Villa's real head."

"What are you going to do with it?"

"Give it to the one who should have it."

"You need someone to ride shotgun?"

"I didn't think there was a chance in the world you'd agree, or I would have asked."

"I want to come," Bud said. "Finish right. Like we started. Just you and me."

"That's great," I said, and meant it.

41

WE took our time, ambling slowly down toward New Mexico and, eventually, to the border.

Along the way, we did some sightseeing—hung out in taverns hosting good musicians. I started drinking again.

Bud was tapering off the cigarettes. I tried to follow his example on that front.

One night, I also tried to buy him a woman.

He wasn't going for it. "I can't pay for that," he said.

"I'm paying," I said.

"I mean that I can't pay for sex. It's … not something I can do under those circumstances. Couldn't perform. It wouldn't be any good, Hector."

"We're men, Bud," I said. "The worst we ever have is fine. And you know, this gal I'll find for you, she's a pro. She's paid to let you be you."

"That's … abhorrent."

I decided, pretty quickly then, it was best not to push.

We drove on.

The box was waiting for me at the hardware store.

We took Pancho's mummified head and stopped at my hacienda to spend the night. I hid the head in the wheel well of my Chevy again.

My place was quiet … dusty. I didn't sleep too good.

Bud sat up reading the draft of my new novel—background for his article, he said.

In the morning we set off for *la Quinta* Luz.

* * *

Pancho Villa purportedly had many women—many "marriages."

But there's really only one woman who is recognized by most as his "official" wife.

Hell, Pancho himself seemed to regard her as his one true woman.

They married in 1914, when she was a girl of twenty.

I had called ahead about our reason for coming. On the phone, she told me that a local priest who married them asked Pancho to first declare his sins. He refused, saying that that would "take days." My kind of groom.

Pancho set Luz Corral Vda. De Villa up in this big, old house in Chihuahua City called *Quinta de Luz*. The French-style house is two stories tall and stuccoed pink. It is made of brown stone and has forty rooms and an open center courtyard. In that courtyard, squatting under the trees heavy with fruit, is the bullet-riddled black Dodge that her husband died in—shot to death while leaving another wedding.

The widow's house is rambling, crumbling and wonderful. My own place back in New Mexico would fit inside, twice.

Luz had turned the house into a museum to her late husband.

She stood by her legendary husband through his incessant sexual betrayals. She accumulated the memorabilia and detritus of his crazed life. And now, seventy-four-years-old and in astonishingly good health, she lived with the slain general's memory all around her.

Such unwarranted devotion made me wonder: where do callous bastards like Villa and me go to find such women?

Villa's luck, I could only suppose, was simply so much better than my own. I hadn't found a devoted caretaker for me or for my memory … not yet.

We rang the bell and Luz Corral de Villa personally answered the door.

"So many," she said, "they try to *fool* me. I hope you are not like them."

"No," I said. "We want no money. We want nothing but to give him back to you so he can rest at last."

We went inside into the cool from the punishing sun. The floors were covered in expensive Italian tile. The old bandit seemingly liked to live well.

Pancho Villa's hats and gun belts hung on the walls.

Myriad photos hung on the walls, too. Photos of Pancho on his mare; standing with Black Jack Pershing (that cocksucker Rodolfo Fierro peering over Villa's left shoulder). Pistols were displayed in glass cases. It was really all more than the eye could absorb.

She led us to a sitting room and I gently deposited the carpetbag on an overstuffed French divan. Luz approached the bag, slowly and carefully.

She opened it and pulled out the head, wrapped in that Navaho rug. She unbundled it, her eyes glistening.

The old woman picked the head up in her wrinkled hands and examined it.

She began to weep and she kissed its forehead.

I turned my gaze away, unable to watch her—it felt like an invasion. I looked at Bud. He looked away from her and from me, his eyes wet.

She placed the head on a table and then kissed my hands with those old lips—the lips that had just kissed the head of Pancho Villa.

She said *gracias* over and over.

I kept saying *de nada*.

The widow bustled over and hugged Bud, then came back and kissed my hands again.

The little widow offered to pay us. Hell, she had no money except pesos from those who came to tour the house.

We refused.

She offered us lunch. I was sorely tempted to stay and hear some stories about Villa, but she kept casting glances at her husband's long-lost head.

"It would be wonderful. But we really must go," I lied.

She looked around, wringing her hands. Then she went to a display case.

She pulled out a set of spurs.

"My husband's favorites." She handed one to me and the other spur to Bud.

"Don't say no," she said. "It's the least we can give you for bring-ing Pancho home."

42

IT seemed wrong to be dissolute—to wander through cantinas and to drink and carouse after that exchange with Pancho Villa's one, true widow. We certainly couldn't do any of that in his own town.

So we crossed the border bridge again.

We pulled up in front of my house.

It was not good to be home.

Bud retrieved his long-languishing, rented Buick from my garage. He had been given another assignment for *True*. The editors wanted him to profile Mickey Spillane. In a rare fit of self-restraint, I kept my opinion to myself.

Bud said, "I'll try to get down here again, come the fall, if you'll have me, Hector. Maybe we could drive down to Galveston Bay … do some deep-sea fishing. You, me and a boat."

"Sounds good," I said. "I'd really like that."

"Hell, it sounds *wonderful*," he said.

We both knew it would never happen.

The young poet left and I stood there alone in my driveway, watching the dust kicked up by his tires slowly sift back down.

Hemingway's phone number weighed heavily in my wallet.

Perhaps I'd finally make that call … inveigle an invitation to Cuba. So many years had passed, maybe we could recapture that old vibe. I took a breath, pulled out the slip of paper with his number, and dialed the operator.

43

EXCERPT *from* True Magazine, *October 1957*:

LASSITER:
A PORTRAIT OF THE ARTIST
AS "CRIME WRITER"

BY Eskin "B." Fiske

Self-described "crime writer" Hector Lassiter lives in the last house in New Mexico, so close to the Rio Grande he could toss his empties in the river from the window above his Smith and Corona typewriter.

The trap for all writers who enter the public consciousness as in the river from the window above his Smith and Corona typewriter.

The trap for all writers who enter the public consciousness as Lassiter has—as, say, a Hemingway has—is the tendency on the part of passionate fans to confuse their favorite writers with the characters that they have created.

That tendency is particularly tough if you are Hector Mason Lassiter, now 57, who came up through the old pulp magazines and occasional scripts for radio crime dramas. His characters include boxers, hard-drinking private detectives and cops, hired killers and desperate men whose lives fall apart in squalid hotels awash in flickering neon that strobes through slitted shades. Often, these men smoke and drink too much. Lassiter's men routinely take and hand out savage beatings most mere mortals wouldn't survive.

Lassiter, the man and the writer, stands in stark contrast to the rogue males about whom he has written in a string of classic crime novels that have shaped and defined the genre.

Each morning at five, Hector Lassiter rises and brews a pot of strong, black Cuban coffee—a brand he developed a taste for while living many years ago in Key West. As his pungent coffee brews, Hector Lassiter shadow boxes and punishes himself with a frenetic series of sit-ups, push-ups and leg lifts.

(cont. on pg. 45)

LASSITER:
A PORTRAIT... (cont. from pg. 12)

Then he writes.

"Three hours a day, minimum," Lassiter told me, sitting in his big study filled with his own books and the books of a few others whom he respects. "Rain or shine, holidays or funerals, there are no exceptions or excuses. On a good day—a really good day—I may do five hours."

Midday in extreme southern New Mexico is like hell in the off-season—"sweltering" doesn't cover it, and talk of a "dry heat" will get your ass kicked. So Hector Lassiter usually naps, then showers and eats a light lunch. Afternoons are spent reading and revising his morning's output. That takes perhaps another two hours.

Then it's time for relaxation: the bull- or cockfights in Juárez, drinks with matador friends and fellow aficionados, or entertaining the more comely Hollywood stars he now moves among as one of Tinsel Town's most sought after screenwriters. Ava Gardner, Carol Baker, Marilyn—he's been spotted with all of them on his arm.

One of his longtime friends is Marlene Dietrich; both deny persistent rumors of an affair. But Lassiter admits the German-born actress/singer probably knows him better than any other woman—certainly better, he says, a little ruefully, than his first three wives.

"Hector is too easily misunderstood," Dietrich argues. "He is like Papa (Hemingway) in that way. He writes so cleanly and with such masculine voice and absolute authority that the subtle art of his writing is often missed. Hector is so much more than a crime writer, but reviewers haven't learned that yet. Since his first novel appeared in 1925, he has been giving us pictures of life as it truly is in our cities, in our outposts and in the American West. And it is interesting to me, interesting and funny and even a little bit sad, that his very best short stories have no crime in them at all.

"Like Hemingway," Marlene Dietrich continued, "he has this other terrible talent—you find yourself warped or transformed by his writing. You find yourself speaking in the cadence and language of his characters. In his presence, you sometimes feel like a character in one of his books."

Actor and director Orson Welles agrees. On the set of Touch of Evil, where Lassiter was visiting as a consultant, Welles said, "Hector, really, is the last of that great breed of martial men steeped in the Western Canon and wholly committed to the craft of writing. I put him in that same vanishing class as a Kipling. A Bierce. Oh, and Hemingway, of course."

Lassiter's military record is at once transparent and mysterious. At age 15, he lied about his age and enlisted. Soon he was chasing the Mexican general Pancho Villa, riding behind Black Jack Pershing.

Following an injury in a skirmish in the high country when a part of the Punitive Expedition, Lassiter shipped out to Europe, eventually to serve as an ambulance driver along the Italian front. It was there that he met his longtime friend Ernest Hemingway. Hemmingway was slightly older and treated Lassiter as a kid brother.

After the war, when many writers of his generation were still finding their way to Paris, Lassiter instead relocated to Key West, where Hemingway would later join him. Like his present house—a sprawling hacienda in La Mesilla—Lassiter's Key West house was barely in the United States. "I like living on the edge, I suppose," he said. "Key West was practically like living in the tropics. Prohibition wasn't, down there. It was bohemian. It rained every day. I love the rain. But then Flagler and that ****sucker FDR ruined Key West ... turned it into a tourist trap ... tried to build that damned highway and rail line. It was time to get out.".

But there were also dark rumors of gun-running and rum-running, the smuggling of refugees from Cuba into the United States.

Next came Seattle, another last American outpost. There, Lassiter lived on an island in Puget Sound. But he sold that cabin in 1941 when he left for Europe to cover the Second World War for a score of major magazines, news agencies and overseas newspapers. There, Lassiter was dogged by rumors of engaging in more than journalism. Some embittered correspondents whom he scooped claimed that Lassiter endangered their protected status by carrying firearms and secretly spying on behalf of Allied Intelligence Agencies. There have even been rumors of his having organized his own band of guerilla fighters during the final fight to liberate Paris. Confronted with these rumors, Lassiter said, with typical laconic good cheer, "Bull****."

In 1946, Hector Lassiter finally made his way back home. He moved as close to the Mexican border as he could and still maintain American residency. There he built his present home.

His newest novel is titled The Land of Dread and Fear—a wrenching study of Texas-Mexico tensions and lonely men confronting mortality along that border.

"These days, all days, I seem to be drawn to the borderlands," Lassiter said. We were sitting in a back room of a cantina on the outskirts of Ciudad Juárez at the time. "The Land of Dread and Fear exemplifies that inchoate obsession of mine," he said.

Lassiter will be staying in La Frontera for his next project: he's agreed to supply the script for a film by legendary director Sam Ford. The cyclopean auteur is working on a movie he's dubbed Rooster of Heaven, a hard-bitten tale of cockfighting and other "bloodsports" to be filmed on location in Ciudad Juárez and Tijuana. The promise of location shooting is what sold Lassiter on the project.

"It's important to me, and to the audience, to see Mexico how she is, not as we would wish her to be. We need to see the squalor ... the deprivation that drives her people—people like Marita, the young, unwed mother in my new novel—to risk everything cross-

crossing the Sonoran Desert, or trying to swim the Rio Grande. We need to see those real Mexican faces, to hear authentic voices. It turns my stomach every time I see Wallace Beery playing Pancho Villa as a drunken lout in a ridiculous suit of lights. The real Villa, love him or detest him, was a nuanced and complex creature and a military genius. He was a man who never drank and in fact banned alcohol in his native province. He was a passionate land reformer and a man committed to literacy and the education of children.

"We don't want to see the real Mexico, or its people," Lassiter continued. "How many of the sad people who read those damned movie magazines remember that Rita Hayworth ain't really Rita Hayworth? Her real name is Margarita Cansino. She was born south of the border. The Hollywood types plucked her hairline to give her a more 'American' forehead. They dyed her hair red and they put her on impossible diets. You think Lupe Velez is really the typical Mexican woman? I can tell you she isn't."

A young Mexican actress on the set of Touch of Evil has read many of Hector Lassiter's books. She read them before she met the man on the set of the film in which she makes her debut. She told your correspondent, "There is an old saying: 'Trust the art, not the artist.' Mr. Hemingway, he has his own version: 'It is a dangerous thing to know a writer.' Mr. Lassiter exudes charisma. He robs rooms of their oxygen. He listens to what people say. So few people really listen to one another now—not just the words, you understand, but the spaces and messages between the words, underlying them. I think it is a little dangerous to read Hector Lassiter and then to come to know him, even a little. When you do that, and then you go back and read his books again, well, it makes one more than a little sad. But he loves my country—particularly its women. I suspect if he can be said to have one great regret, it might be that he was not born Mexican. I suspect he would have preferred to have ridden with Pancho Villa instead of after him."

44

BUD Fiske's profile of me made me laugh—for about a minute.

At first flush, I wished every word was ... well, *True*.

Then it made me sad. Maybe even a bit angry.

Like all profiles, it didn't really catch me: my truculence; my selfishness; my tendency to try too hard to please. Well, to please pretty women, anyway.

So I read the piece two more times and realized that Fiske's profile of me was, at base, a minefield—a series of carefully couched signals. Signals sent by Fiske, of course, but also perhaps by Marlene and by Orson Welles, if their quotes were at all accurate. Perhaps they were not. Mine certainly weren't. But then, I'd encouraged Fiske to make it all up anyway.

But it was more than that. It was Bud Fiske trying to assign me some social relevance regarding issues and topics I assumed to be of importance to Bud. For surely they weren't my causes. Some of it portrayed me as the crusader I could only guess Fiske wished or was trying to will me to be.

And Marlene and Orson claimed a *gravitas* for my "oeuvre" that it didn't deserve and I didn't intend for it.

I suspected that the editors of *True* must have been disappointed with the piece. It ran shorter than most they published and ended abruptly. It was as though someone setting type said, "Enough of this somber, self-important bullshit."

In the previous February's issue, *True* did a major "book-length" profile of Hemingway as seen by his "friends and enemies." I'd gotten a call or two for quotes, but resisted. Probably just as well—the article was edgy and bitchy. I'm sure that Hemingway must have hated the thing.

But the editors, and most of their readers, I suspect, must have loved that sucker.

With me they'd gotten this hagiography—worse, a sanctimonious distortion—there among the adverts for Carling Black Label Beer, Weaver Scopes, Starcraft boats and Norm Thompson's "Adventure" boots. There among breathless articles on the Cleveland Headhunter and the semi-nude photos of Anita Ekberg. I threw the magazine down in disgust.

I couldn't bear my lonely house. I put on a stack of Marlene's records, but every song ripped through me—"Illusions," "Let's Call It A Day" and "Something I Dreamed Last Night."

Every day brought stinging rain—the remnants of Hurricane Audrey.

Things weren't good down south, either—a massive earthquake had struck Mexico City and killed scores.

So I climbed into my dusty Chevy and drove until I hit El Paso.

I ambled around town for a while; stood and looked at the place where Bud and me had "found" his cowboy hat. It made me feel even lonelier. I missed the scrawny cocksucker so much it surprised me.

After a time, I asked directions to the nearest whorehouse.

I paid forty dollars for a pretty young Mexican thing who was just "finding her feet," so to speak, in the life. Maybe it was the diabetes. Maybe it was my age (or hers). Hell, maybe it was some flavor of new-found scruples.

Whatever it was, I just couldn't.

Her mouth and her youth, her black eyes and hair, her small, pert breasts and lush hips, everything she had—well, it wasn't enough for me.

So I sat there in her sad, dirty bed for an hour, talking to her, listening to her story. I tried in my best storyteller's fashion to talk her out of that dead-end life she'd chosen for herself, and into mine.

She wasn't going for my pitch.

I didn't know which one of us that said less for.

My time up, I dressed and stumbled across the street to the VFW Hall.

I flashed my card at the wounded, drunken gatekeeper at the door and he waved me in with his remaining arm.

It was dark and cool inside—a wanton womb for old and broken men. The air was laced with blue-gray streams of cigarette smoke and reeked of beer. Buddy Loy Burke was playing on the jukebox: "Soldier's Lament." Felt like home. Then someone dropped coins for Marlene Dietrich: "I May Never Go Home Anymore." Now it *was* just like home.

Now it was just me and all the other old campaigners—sitting there with their eye patches, missing legs and their hooks-for-hands.

There were veterans from all the brand-name wars: World War I, World War II, Korea ... maybe even a few from the Pershing Expedition. There were a few others who must have been roped into other, perhaps clandestine conflicts that never achieved marquee status.

Sitting in the corner was one ancient man, whom I guessed for a bonafide Civil War vet—probably the last of the bugle boys. He was in a wheel chair. I took the table next to his. The bartender called to me across the room, "What'll it be, Ace?"

I fished out my Zippo and a pack of Pall Malls. I said, "Scotch, neat. And make the first one a double."

The Civil War vet sipped his beer and said, "Hard liquor—that'll kill you faster than anything, sonny."

I smiled and blew some smoke. "Promise?"

There was an old piano in the corner. When the jukebox played out, I moved over there and sat down. I play a little. I began banging out "Canción Mixteca." I began to sing the Spanish lyrics by José López Alavés. He was a Mixtec Indian who hailed from Oaxaca:

How far I am from the land where I was born
Immense sadness fills my thoughts
I see myself so alone and so sad
Like a leaf in the wind
I would like to cry, I would like to die
From the feeling
Land of the sun
I long to see you
Now that I live so far from your light, without love
I see myself so alone and so sad
Like a leaf in the wind.

An old Mexican who had volunteered to fight with us in World War II picked up his flamenco guitar and accompanied me. He was missing an important finger on his right hand, yet played beautifully. Another old Mexican vet who crossed the border to fight Hitler picked up his accordion.

Soon, every veteran in the joint was singing with me. I'd almost reached the end of the song when I realized that I was crying.

BOOK TWO

1967:
THE
LAND OF DREAD
AND FEAR

ADIOS

01

TEN years ... *gone.*

I'm old and tired and used up.

I've lived too long. Gone and outlived my sorry-ass world.

It's been two years since I've written anything worth a damn.

This morning I read a list of the best-selling books of the year. I wasn't on it. The stuff that was? Books by these characters named Styron, Potok, Uris and Kazan. Poetry, according to the list, seems to be crap written by this dude, Rod McKuen. The really big sellers this year? *Rosemary's Baby* by Ira Levin and Phyllis Diller's *Marriage Manual.*

Like I said, ain't much of real worth around anymore.

My daughter is still dead.

My country has gone to hell.

Our last two Democrat presidents have led us into another war—but not the kind of conflict that a scheming mercenary like Emil Holmdahl would ever find a way to turn a buck on. In this dark year of our gone-missing Lord, only the industrial military complex gets rich on warfare. It's what the country gets for electing some dumbass, jug-eared, appendectomy-scar-flaunting Texas politician to be president—"great frontiers" and a shadow government; black budgets and bigger bombs. Or maybe JFK and LBJ just figured the time had come to salt the street corners with a fresh crop of begging, one-legged and one-armed men—boys with burned faces and missing eyes and noses.

Those World War II and Korean War vets *were* starting to get long in the tooth.

Either way, it's all gone away now.

Kids are growing their hair long and burning the flag and blowing up their schools. Women are burning their underwear.

I don't recognize the stuff on the radio as music. Whatever happened to Marty Robbins or Sonny James or Buddy Loy Burke?

My *Black Mask* stablemates are all dead. Lester Dent, the most decent, the most *civilized*, of us, died of a heart attack in March 1959. Chandler died March 26 of the same year in California. Hammett went nuts and communist and clocked out in January 1961 in New York. Dash was destitute and eaten up by lung cancer.

Ernest Hemingway, the Great Ape of American literature, shot himself in Idaho in the summer of 1961. Thank God we patched it up before he picked up that gun. Hem was old and sick and deprived of everything he loved. When word reached me in July of that year that Papa had decapitated himself with his shotgun, I fired up a Pall Mall with his engraved gift lighter and poured a second glass of Rioja and set it out for Papa's ghost. But he wasn't thirsty that day; so I drank it for him. I understand why he took himself out. I understand it more every day. It's a terrible kind of wisdom and it's too late to do anything with it.

My hands shake now and I don't see too good.

Diabetes and cataracts—they're an unbeatable tag team.

My caretaker—or fifth "wife" as she thinks of herself—sees to it that I'm deprived the cigarettes and liquor that would at least make these last days of mine maybe something like bearable.

The bedsheet falls flat just below my right knee where my leg now ends. I'm getting the strong sense that the sawbones has designs on my left leg, too. *Fuck him*—I'll shoot myself first. The old Colt lays loaded and waiting under my pillow. I'll turn it on myself one day … one day soon, perhaps.

In the meantime, I think a lot about walking.

It's been ten years and a few months since all that bloody business with Pancho Villa's head—another of my reckless whims that went very wrong.

Emil Holmdahl died on April 8, 1963. Nearly eighty, the old soldier of fortune was loading his car for a planned prospecting trip deep down in Mexico. Maybe he wanted to take another swing at our bogus map written in ammonia by Bud Fiske. Holmdahl suffered a massive stroke and died moments later. At least the bastard went out on both feet. The old head plunderer was buried in a crypt with his wife. I'm betting that tomb has got big strong locks and thick doors to keep the headhunters at bay.

Prescott Bush is still on the right side of the sod—*that fucker* still gets around. He was born in central Ohio; he spent years in the hardware business in Missouri; he was senator from Connecticut from 1952 to 1963. No shocker here—he was a Yale University trustee. He's since left politics and gone into banking back East. Word has it he's grooming his sons and grandsons to follow the family path into politics. May your God help us all.

Like Emil, I'd bet good money that Prescott will take exceptional steps to keep his bones intact when they finally plant the tight-assed bastard.

Orson Welles never steered another film into port with his artistic vision intact. The suits and the bean counters dicked poor Orson at every turn, mutilated every movie he tried to make after *Citizen Kane*. He's been reduced to voice-overs and guest shots on *I Love Lucy*—a talk show regular who performs dime store magic tricks for Mike Douglas and Merv Griffin.

Marie Magdalena von Losch—Marlene Dietrich, the Kraut—she made one other real movie after *Touch of Evil*. That was *Judgment at Nuremberg*. It paled next to Orson Welles' disfigured noir classic. She's performing in nightclubs, but I don't get around much anymore. So we talk on the phone, we exchange letters. She misses Papa and he dominates our conversations. The Kraut says, "It's the friends you can call up at four a.m. that matter." She and me, we never speak in daylight.

Last night I couldn't sleep and called her—she serenaded me to sleep with an *a cappella* rendition of "La Vie En Rose."

Luz Corral is still alive—holed-up in that big, old house/museum full of Pancho Villa memorabilia. She claims she'll live a hundred years. Stranger things have happened.

Eskin "Bud" Fiske: poet, sometimes country music lyricist, outsider writer. Screenwriter, raconteur, essayist, *busker*. Pop culture celebrity. He turns up in cameos on dumbass TV comedies and talk shows. I caught him on that loopy Bob Conrad TV series the other night, *The Wild Wild West*. It was some outlandish episode starring Bud and his Rat Pack buddies Sammy and Peter Lawford—JFK's debauched brother-in-law.

Good ol' Bud—son of a bitch can still turn a hell of a phrase when he's pressed too.

Alicia … I sometimes lose an evening staring at the one photo I have of her. She's well … her and her *children*.

So it ends here. I can hear my Brit "wife" now, speaking with this journalist come to interview me. It's likely my last interview. That suits me just fine.

I switch off the shortwave radio—a mariachi station I seem to be parked on these days. The last tune was by a woman singer performing Rita Arvizu's "Ejercito Militar."

"Wifey" is reading my last scribe the riot act now—no booze, no coffin nails.

Holy Jesus, another trip down memory lane for some goddamned reporter looms. Thank Christ it's the last.

My tale of Pancho Villa's head, the last true tale I'll ever spin, ends here.

So it's *adios*, partner … *vaya con dios.*

To better days.

Maybe we'll see you down some other world's road, buckaroo.

DÍA DE LOS MUERTOS

02

EXCERPT from the *El Paso Herald Post*, dated Wednesday, November 1, 1967:

—THE EL PASO HERALD POST—WEDNESDAY

MYSTERY AUTHOR FOUND DEAD IN BIZARRE MURDER/SUICIDE

BY RUSSELL HARDIN

Sheriff Dave Duhan said Lassiter,

IN BIZARRE MURDER/SUICIDE

BY RUSSELL HARDIN
Herald Staff Writer

Journalist suspected of slaying last of the great Pulp writers

---

Celebrated crime novelist Hector Mason Lassiter was found shot to death in his own bed yesterday afternoon.

The body of Lassiter and that of his presumed slayer were found by the author's wife, Hannah Lassiter, and their housekeeper, Carmelita Magón. The two women found the corpses when they returned from a brief shopping trip near the couple's home in La Mesilla, New Mexico.

Lassiter's presumed killer is Andrew Nagel, a Chicago-based freelance journalist who'd driven cross-country to interview the famous mystery writer for a magazine article.

Sheriff Dave Duhan said Lassiter, who had recently undergone the amputation of his right leg as a result of complications from diabetes, was found dead as the result of a single gunshot wound to the stomach.

Lassiter's suspected slayer, Nagel, age 22, apparently killed himself with a single shot to the head from the same weapon: a vintage, 1873-model Colt Peacemaker.

"It's a real museum piece," Sheriff Duhan said. "The gun belonged to Hector Lassiter, who often slept with the revolver under his pillow for security, according to his widow. We suspect that Nagel wrestled the gun from Lassiter and gut shot him with it, then turned the Colt on himself."

The sheriff said there were signs of a fierce struggle; the remnants of several broken cosmetic bottles were scattered across the bed and an adjacent nightstand.

"It's frustrating," Duhan said, "because there are some tantalizing potential clues that have been lost to us." Those clues, he elaborated, would likely have come from a tape recorder found with the two bodies. The reel-to-reel recording machine belonged to the journalist and appeared to have been running for some time.

Any possibility of recovering any conversation, or any sounds of the struggle and shootings, was "erased" when the gun was twice turned on the tape machine, the sheriff said.

Despite doctor's orders to the contrary, and strict instructions from Mrs. Lassiter, the journalist appears to have shared several cigarettes and a

(cont. from pg. +)

bottle of liquor with the ailing author.

The door to the bedroom/murder scene was found locked from the inside when Mrs. Lassiter and her housekeeper returned home.

Two mysterious initials were also scrawled in blood above the author's bed: "E.Q."

Sheriff Duhan said that several handwritten letters sent to Lassiter by fellow author Estelle Quartermain—a British mystery author, whom, ironically enough, is famed for her own so-called "locked-room" mysteries—were found by the victim's bedside. Perhaps significantly, Nagel had interviewed Dame Estelle Quartermain several weeks before soliciting the interview with Hector Lassiter.

Sheriff Duhan refused to comment on any possible connection, or to divulge the contents of the letters. Repeated calls to Dame Quartermain went unreturned.

Mrs. Lassiter also refused to speak with the Herald. There are as yet unconfirmed reports that she is engaged in a bitter legal dispute concerning her late husband's estate. Lassiter's will, according to attorney Hobie Meed, left the bulk of his estate—including the home in La Mesilla—to his client, former actress Alicia Vicente, and her three children. A second home, located in Key West, Florida, was left to Hannah Lassiter.

When contacted for a comment about his death, longtime Lassiter friend Marlene Dietrich, famed German-born actress and chanteuse, said simply, "He was a hell of a man. What more than that can I say that would matter a damn? When you're dead, you're dead. End of your story."

Another longtime friend, noir poet and Hollywood Squares regular Eskin "Bud" Fiske said, "Hec was the last great one ... the last true writer of the old Black Mask school. I hope they have enough room in Valhalla for the magnificent (expletive deleted)."

Fiske then added, somewhat cryptically, "And I find it very significant that some hophead from Yale took Hector out. That doesn't go unnoticed by me. And I mean to look into that a bit more myself. 'Prescott' will know what I mean."

Fiske resisted repeated requests by this reporter to elaborate on his rather bizarre statement, or to explain to whom the name "Prescott" referred.

Sheriff Duhan, however, did confirm that a syringe and heroin were indeed found among Nagel's personal effects recovered from the Lassiters' guestroom. He also confirmed that both of Nagel's forearms were covered with old and new needle scars. "He was a longtime and frequent heroin abuser," Duhan said. The sheriff also confirmed that Nagel was indeed a Yale graduate, "Although I frankly fail to see what that has to do with anything," Duhan said.

Funeral arrangements are being determined.

Hector Lassiter was pre-deceased by a toddler daughter, Dolores, who died of complications of a congenital heart defect in April 1956.

His fourth wife, Maria Lassiter, died of an apparent heroin overdose in New Mexico on May 13, 1956.

LA CABEZA DE HÉCTOR LASSITER

03

EXCERPT from the *El Paso Herald Post,* dated Saturday, November 1, 1970:

Author's grave robbed and corpse mutilated

(cont. from pg. 18)

Local authorities are continuing the investigation into the robbing of crime novelist/screenwriter Hector Lassiter's grave on Halloween night.

The grave was found uncovered and the coffin pried open. The body of Lassiter was found partially exposed and decapitated. The head of the famed author—the victim of a bizarre murder three years ago to the day—remains missing.

Authorities say they are baffled as

BOOK THREE

1970:
THE
WASTELAND

01

BUD Fiske, speaking.

Perhaps local authorities really were baffled.

But I wasn't.

And I owed Hector.

I'd spent too many years away from my friend after the late 1950s. Always meant to get down to that big, old, beautiful and sad hacienda in New Mexico. But my own career was taking off then.

So I delayed.

I procrastinated.

I figured, *there's always tomorrow.*

But one day there isn't—just a string of successive, unsatisfactory todays and mounting yesterdays that mean to bury you.

Hector and I stayed in touch, exchanged letters and phone calls. We sent one another inscribed first editions of our respective works.

Hector floated some of the script work he no longer had the heart or stamina for my way and got me through some lean times.

Then I became a kind of half-assed pop culture celebrity, waxing while Hector waned.

I became a second-string Rat Pack member.

I scored voice-overs on *Underdog*, frequent guest shots on Carson and Merv Griffin, *Laugh-In* gags and *The Hollywood Squares*. And that fucking cameo on *The Wild Wild West* with Bobby Conrad, Sammy Davis Jr. and that whack-job Peter Lawford—the fucker who clawed out my right eye at the series' wrap party in 1969.

When Hector went down under Nagel's gun in 1967, I almost went after the Skull and Bones right then. But there were enough odd, attendant angles to stay my hand. The stuff with Estelle Quartermain vibed something very close to credible. Maybe the junkie journalist *really did* take Hector out as a result of unfathomable loyalty or fucked-up fealty to the daffy old Brit mystery maven.

Through channels, I heard dirty secrets about the letters written by Quartermain that were found by Hector's bed, about Hector's "crude" annotations on the letters, indicating he'd bedded a drunken Dame Quartermain at a party many years before—shaming her husband and embarrassing the "Queen of the Locked Room Mystery."

So I waited.

I *watched*.

I came to think Nagel's Yale credentials were just some spooky coincidence.

And, hell, you know what? They may be.

But then the rotten cocksuckers broke into the Orogrande graveyard and hacked off my best friend's head.

Then I *knew*.

And then I went for them.

02

IT'S raining hard in Connecticut tonight.

I've dialed around the radio and found myself a country station. Buddy Loy Burke is crooning now. He was Hector's favorite singer/songwriter and it's maybe an omen—a cover of "Ghost Riders in the Sky."

The roads and sidewalks are slick with a thick layer of sodden leaves. The "Tomb," the gray, imposing sanctum sanctorum of the dumbass Yale Skull and Bones Society, squats sinisterly under bare-limbed trees and forked tongues of lightning. It looks like a high-end mausoleum.

I pull over two blocks past their HQ. Before heading in, just in case things get rough, I take out my glass eye and put it in a small velvet pouch on the passenger's seat. I tug on my despised, black eye patch. I only hope to hell I don't have to shoot anyone. I'm still adjusting to the one eye—my compromised depth perception plays hell with my pool game and marksmanship.

This time, I know some more things about this "secret society" of "Bonesmen" than we knew in 1957. Getting that information cost someone dear. (Look for a Skull and Bones member, class of '66. He's got two black eyes and a new limp, tall, horse-faced, too much hair— like Andrew Jackson's latter-day, sour-faced love child, maybe.)

Inside the Tomb, they run things five minutes ahead of the rest of the world.

For the record, Jesus, I do so hate this dipshit, secret hand-shake stuff.

Thursdays and Sundays they gather in the "Firefly Room" for dinner at 6:30, their time.

So now I wait outside, wearing a black slouch hat and draped in a long, black great coat that obscures the sawed-off .410 underneath. I have a holdout derringer tucked up my right sleeve and two chrome-plated .45s thrust down my waistband. It's a little after eight now in the real world. They don't drink in the Tomb (some stupefying prohibition that even Yale's myriad and chicken-shit hard-partying secret societies observe), so by 8:15 p.m. (their time), they get thirsty and go wander off campus to get plastered.

Dinner's breaking up. I let a few Bonesmen pass by. Then I grab a lone straggler. I press my shotgun to his belly. He checks my face; looks like maybe he half-ass knows me from somewhere, but can't quite place me. (Goddamned *Hollywood Squares!*)

He's perhaps foxed by the eye patch. And in these environs, that wicked black patch makes even *me* look like some flavor of bad ass.

I explain, tersely and quietly, what I want—to be escorted to the "Trophy" room where they keep Geronimo's skull. Where they would have put Pancho's noggin. Where I'm sure they have squir-reled away Hector Lassiter's stolen head.

Dig this shitty, spooky ambience—*Jesus*, so dark; like some frat boy's vision of Anton LeVay's West Coast fuck pad.

I hear voices up ahead in what they call the "Inner Temple," or room "322." I hear a young man's twang. I duck in, steal a glance at the speaker, and duck back. The voice comes from a guy with big ears, a medium build and Texas accent. He's emphatic. "This is just diseased," the young guy says. "Christ, what the hell is the fascination with this sick stuff? What a bunch of major-league assholes you all are."

An impatient, older voice now: "Quiet, Temporary. We asked you back for this because your grandfather couldn't travel and this is important to him—as you well know. And your poor father. How in hell could he lose that senate seat to fucking Lloyd Bentsen? He must be devastated. I know that I am." A pause, then, "You know, Temporary, what Villa's head meant to *Mog*. This drunken scribbler Lassiter cost us another chance at acquiring Villa's head. It was important for a member of your family to be here for the installation ceremony. Even if it is only you."

"Fuck this," the returned Skull and Bones member dubbed "Temporary" says. He grouses on, "And drop the 'Temporary' nickname. You know I don't go for this secret handshake and handles crap. Never have. And I really gotta get back to the Guard base."

The older voice again: "To hell with that. It's only the Texas 'Champagne Unit.' You'll leave when we're ready for you to go, Temporary."

A snort. "'Temporary.' It's 'George.' 'George W.' Short and simple, yeah?"

"You mock and sully us," the older man says. "For decades we've chased Villa's skull, and this bastard, this boozing, pulp magazine writer, took it from us when we almost had it in our grasp again. That Mexican barbarian invaded the United States and killed Americans. Now we avenge that."

"Christ's sake," this George W. says, "you avenge all that by putting some other poor bastard's rotting skull in a glass case? How exactly does that work? *Man.* It makes no sense at all. It's never made sense—not even taking Villa's head. None of it makes a lick of sense."

The old man: "Granted, the Punitive Expedition failed in its central aims. We—"

George W. cuts the old bastard off. "Whatever made any of 'em think sending Jack Pershing and all those soldiers south of the border would accomplish anything? Hell, it's a crazy-ass notion—getting some wild hair and chasing a single man in another country's desert. Especially a man whose countrymen are bent on protecting him. Hell's belles, even the ones that hated Villa covered for him. The Mexicans, to a man, saw Pershing as an invader, not an avenger. The Pershing Expedition was a farce. Pure folly. It just genned-up anti-American sentiment in the Mexicans. President Wilson would have been ahead to pay some of Pancho's cronies to take him out or turn him in. But to send Pershing and the Army in? Nuts, man. Just nuts. Like Teddy Roosevelt and that Berber chieftain—where was President Roosevelt's good counsel that time out? Same thing with Wilson, sending Pershing into Mexico—wrong-headed and shortsighted. It was just vengeful."

"It matters to your grandfather," the old man says. "Probably matters to your father, to 'Poppy.' And my God, I sincerely hope you don't follow them into politics. Not with these naïve, simpleton notions of yours."

George says, "You're one major-league asshole, you know that? It doesn't matter to me—none of this dipshit mumbo-jumbo and secret crap does. It's just damned nonsense and so much horseshit. My father has always seen the world in shades of gray and, you know, nuance is the father of hesitation. And, hell, you're just a bunch of grave robbers. You defiled a fellow

American's grave, taking Lassiter's head. So tell me, who's the real evildoer?"

Well hell: that strikes me as an entry line.

I shoulder in, my Skull and Bone's hostage thrust out front. Heads turn, wide-eyed to see a one-eyed invader in their granite and marble hidey-hole.

"Just so you know, up front," I say, "I've got a sawed-off shotgun at this man's back. And I *will* use it."

This old man with a moustache, dressed as Don Quixote, is sitting there looking rusted and rickety. There's another bastard perched there beside the Knight of the Woeful Countenance, dressed in a devil's suit.

Must be initiation night.

The ersatz Quixote is so flummoxed he spits as he says, "Who the hell are you?"

"Nobody," I say. "Just some unwashed nobody with no college degree. But I'm here to pick up a friend. I want Hector Lassiter's head, and *muy pronto.*"

That declaration triggers more bluster from the Don.

George W. shoots the old bastard a look of genuine contempt, then cocks his thumbs at me. "See, this is where this bullshit—this morbid plundering of graves and this vindictiveness—gets all you ghoulish old assholes. I should let him shoot all of you."

"Where's my friend's head?"

George W. waves at a glass cabinet. Maybe five or six skulls and some assorted bones are displayed in there. I try not to look too hard; Hector was my friend—and not in the ground (or out) as long as Villa's head had been when I made that skull's accidental acquaintance. I toss a folded-up carpetbag to George W. and say, "Put it in there for me, would you, Ace?"

George grimaces, but nods. He picks up a couple of folded, red-linen napkins—he's not going to touch the head with his bare hands and who could blame him? He saunters over to the "trophy" cabinet.

Sour-faced, he lowers a not-too-mummified-looking something into the bag and seals it up. I remember Hector long ago lobbing a severed head in a similar bag at a gun-pointing Texas Republican down El Paso way. So I caution George, "Hand it over to me, slowly and carefully."

He does. George smirks and winks. "You've got a pair on you, *amigo.*"

"You know," I say, smiling back, "I didn't think it would be this easy."

George tugs on his ear lobe and bites his lip. Poor bastard's eyebrows meet in the middle. He's going to need to fix that if he really wants to go into politics. "It ain't *that* easy, *hombre,*" he says. "*This* is the easy part. Getting out of here, that likely won't be too tough, either. And you'll have a few minutes' head start. This joint is lousy with intelligence types—past, present and future. They distrust electronics because they all know what they can do with 'em on a surveillance front. So there are no phones here in the Tomb. You'll have a head start—no pun intended—but out there ... well, they can bring a lot of heat to bear on you, *amigo.* I don't envy you the pursuit. Pancho Villa at least had the advantage of the border and several days of running time."

Christ, my new friend George probably has a point. But I brass it out, backing out now, Hector's head in a bag clutched in my left hand, the shotgun leveled in my right. "You said it yourself, George—one man lost on a continent ... it's a fool's mission to try and find him."

George nods and smiles sadly. "But that was a long time ago and in another country. You're back East, *amigo*. Ain't no frontiers left here in the land of the brave and the free."

Argue with *that*. I smile and say, "I hear you." Then, "Thanks for the assist."

Don Quixote: "Temporary is right: we'll crush you, little man."

The Devil: "You can run, but you can't hide. If you run, you'll only die tired. We'll soon have your head in this cabinet. I promise you that."

The last voice I hear is George W.'s, urging me to change cars *often*. His last bit of advice: "Lose that eye patch and fast, partner—damn few pirate look-alikes roaming the Yale campus." It's good, if obvious, counsel. I throw my Skull and Bone's hostage to the floor and back out fast. Outside, I slam the door behind me. Checking to be certain nobody is following, I ditch my black coat and fedora in a trash bin.

I stow Hector's head on the floor behind the front passenger's seat and toss my eye patch out the window. I slap in the glass eye. For old time's sake, I've brought along my old, white *vaquero's* hat—the one Hector took for me from a Texas Republican. It's conspicuous as hell here in the East. But that's the point: "Naked is the best disguise." And a white cowboy hat is 180-degrees out of phase with a black slouch hat. So I put it on.

George's admonition about changing cars eats at me. I palm into the Greyhound lot and park there. I'll let the fuckers chase cross-country buses, assuming they ever identify my car. I snag a cab across town and then hoof it two blocks to a used car lot. About that time, I start to hear and see all the black helicopters. There are maybe a dozen of them hovering, searching.

I wonder what they've been told to look for?

Through the curtain of rain, the choppers all look big and black and unbeatable.

Getting the sweats now, I pay cash up front. Twenty minutes later, I drive off in my new, used, midnight blue '66 Impala with a red replacement hood. She's got a lot under that mismatched hood—a real power car.

I fill up the tank and head southwest—highways all the way.

Twenty-four hours of white-knuckle driving, sustaining myself with gas station coffee, BBF burgers and little pills they sell to truckers.

Twenty-five hours in—heart racing, sweating furiously, hands shaking—I start talking to Hector's head.

More troubling: Hector's head starts talking back.

Hec gives me some advice.

Hector says, *Call Alicia,* now. *Have her meet you somewhere. Tell her to make sure she's not followed.*

I say, *Why?*

Hector says, *Because they are going to expect you to go to New Mexico to put me back together. They'll watch my old place—Alicia's new home.*

Goddamn, Hector's *so* right. I slide off the interstate and drop some quarters. Her phone might be tapped, so I tell Alicia to get to another phone and call me back. She does. I instruct her to cross the border, follow the Rio Grande down to Matamoros. I'll meet her there in a week.

But damned if that wait by the phone for her to call me back doesn't cost me, lets them get a bead on me, somehow—the fucking CIA spooks and their Yale cronies.

Ten minutes down, thinking maybe I finally see some light at the end of this hellish tunnel that I'm locked into, it happens. A sniper on an overpass puts three bullets through my windshield. One goes through my hat, just missing my head. Another misses me, but flying windshield glass nicks my cheeks.

The third bullet takes out my radio. No more country tunes to drive to.

Those *cocksuckers*!

Time for some new wheels.

03

IT'S a zombie's sprint.

No safety.

No hiding.

No sleep.

I'm reduced to running with the bag with Hector's head, a trenchcoat to cover all my guns, a duffel bag filled with wadded up clothes, pills to keep me awake and a thermos filled with black coffee. My left kidney's burning—probably first intimations that I've built for myself a hell of a set of kidney stones with all this undiluted, high-octane java these past few days.

I look like a hollow-eyed bum, unshaven, unshowered.

All those cuts on my face courtesy of the exploding windshield don't make me less conspicuous.

I'm nearly always nauseous from lack of sleep. My junk food, caffeine and pep pill diet is playing hell with my diabetes; the insulin is hard-pressed to compensate.

And some *pachuco* with a big old knife recently left a deep wound in my left arm. I'm watching it, afraid it'll infect. Bandit bastard wasn't good, but he made up for it with feral viciousness and a high tolerance for pain. He must have been hired on the cheap when they somehow got another bead on me in Shreveport. They got their money's worth, whatever they paid him: it took five slugs to his upper torso to take him down for keeps.

It's tantalizingly close now, but I figure the Texas border is too tough for me to cross at checkpoints without *them* picking me off.

I've had an entire nation to hide in and they've nearly gotten me six times in three days. Now that they've located me in Shreveport, I double back a bit—head back east. Then I veer south.

There's a charter boat waiting for me in Morgan City, an old rumrunner with a thirty-footer. He's agreed to take me across the Gulf, despite the fact we run the risk of running right into the eye of a tropical storm.

But you know what? Money really *does* talk. And that's a good thing—it can keep up my end of the conversation, 'cause I figure to spend the next few hours vomiting; I don't do rough seas.

Here's my plan, such as it is:

Hector and me'll track toward the Rio Grande and the old rumrunner will drop me someplace along the Mexican coast.

Then what's left of Hector and me will make our way along the Rio Grande to find Alicia.

Money isn't the only thing talking.

Hector's head is going on, a mile a minute. He likes this plan. And he feels like writing. He starts dictating this tale to me he wants to call *The Big Comb-over*.

It's a new crime novel—a harrowing collision of male-pattern baldness and tattooed treasure maps.

* * *

The boat is a rolling sanctuary. My skipper is a grizzled madman—like the crazy captain who'd run you up the river to search for King Kong or to kill Kurtz.

And what do you know? He's a fellow cyclops—he's got an eye missing on the same side. That shared loss seems to make us brothers in his eye(s?).

Three hours in, he convinces me to go below—to wash up, rest, whatever I want. I take him up on his proposition.

Below, I make the mistake of checking the mirror. *Jesus God* ... I look like a wild-eyed vagrant.

I borrow the skipper's razor and put in a fresh blade and shave for the first time in nearly a week.

I slap on some "borrowed" Old Spice—I'm in deep clover now. I take a whore's bath and wash my hair in the sink. I check my reflection again. Ain't great, but at least I no longer look like Peachey Carnahan in those last few paragraphs of *The Man Who Would Be King*. But like poor Peachey, "I've urgent private affairs—in the south." And just a little left of a friend.

The knife wound in my arm is looking a little better now, and that's a relief. I fear the gangrene.

I slick back my wet hair and change into some "fresh" clothes. I feel almost human. I gaze at the cot ... so inviting.

But then the sea begins to pitch. Rain lashes the cabin's portholes. The storm is on us. Can't sleep through this—hell, I can't cross the room. When the cabin goes nearly 65-degrees sideways,

I start thinking Hector's going to get a burial at sea—and I figure he won't be going under alone.

I curl up in the captain's cot and try to close my eyes. But there is no sleeping through this storm. I see the carpetbag tumble across the floor. I untangle myself from the sheets and toss them carelessly over the pillows on the cot. I retrieve the bag with Hector's head and duck under the steps leading to topside, figuring I'll wedge the bag under the lowest runner to keep it in place. Then I see the feet descending.

I don't remember those *pants.*

It's supposed to be just me and the one-eyed skipper on the boat.

So who is this skulking cocksucker?

He's wearing white slacks and matching white deck shoes with no socks, a cordovan belt and a pressed blue shirt with rolled up sleeves. He's got a twenty-dollar haircut. Sucker looks like an Abercrombie & Fitch catalogue version of a sailor.

I smell Yale—maybe CIA.

He crosses to the cot, closing in on that shadowy pile of pillows and sheets. He goes at the sheets with a big buck knife—a flurry of stabs and feints as he struggles to maintain his footing against the pitch of the ship. I cross behind him like some sleep-deprived drunk—trying to get to my overcoat and my guns. He senses movement, pivots on heel and raises his knife. The ship rolls again, in the opposite direction, and me and my would-be killer slam into the same bulkhead. I shake it off, rising. The impact did the other guy real harm: he's standing there dumbfounded, staring at the knife that's now buried hilt-deep in his own aorta. He drops to his knees, then falls forward, hands at his side, no attempt to break his fall. A dead man's fall. The knife's point digs out a little deeper through his bloodied back.

So I figure I'm gonna be made for this death—nobody's gonna believe that this likely-to-be psychopath, this orders-exceeding frat boy, somehow butter-fingered himself to death.

While the traitorous captain is busy keeping us afloat, I wrap the dead bastard up tight in the bedsheets and get him shouldered up into a fireman's carry. It's hard work with all that dead, loose-limbed weight, with the shifting stairs and a rolling ocean underfoot. But I creep topside behind the captain who is intent and white-knuckled at the wheel. The captain's not seeing and not hearing me.

I pitch Mr. Yale overboard and creep back downstairs. I'm sweating like a pig. I wash up quickly again, change into yet another shirt—an unbloodied shirt—and take a couple shots of the captain's bourbon.

Then I grab my guns, grab Hector's head and head back topside.

My gun pressed tight to the back of the skipper's head, I say, "I hope for your sake we're still headed toward Mexico."

"Not much choice," the one-eyed old man says sourly. "The storm is moving west to east. We're nearly through it, I think. I'm sure as hell not about to go back in. I'll make port in Mexico where I drop you, then head back when it clears."

Uh-huh.

Jesus, I'm so tired. But I sweat out several hours there, my gun pressed to the back of the old bastard's head. He accepted *a hundred dollars* to let them kill me. *I* was paying this cyclopean cocksucker *five hundred* to take me across.

The math slays me.

And that same math may yet slay him.

Fifty yards offshore, I pistol whip the skipper behind his right ear.

I've watched him work the controls for hours now, so I figure I can hit the shoreline just fine on my own.

I line her up and set the controls to go in rather slow.

Or so I think.

I'm shooting for a semi-remote stretch of beach, about a half-mile south of some lights—some fishing village or vacation bungalows, maybe. I climb up on the prow, leaning into the offshore breeze. I have my bags full of guns, my insulin, and Hector in hand—ready to leap when the impact comes.

That "impact"—that's too gentle a word.

It's more like ramming a car into a wall at thirty or forty miles an hour—while you're standing on the hood.

There's something to be said for wet sand, and this is it—*it's too fucking hard.*

I struggle up, seeing lights and now nauseous as hell. I find my bags and start walking toward the real lights strung out along the shoreline.

Then I trip over something, and I fall.

I struggle back up and turn to see what took me down. It's a body—the body of the one-eyed skipper. The luckless sucker shot right through the bridge's window and way out in front of his own boat. He's staring up at me with that one good eye.

Thing is, the rest of him is spread eagle, face down. I'm no doctor, but I'm pretty sure necks aren't supposed to do that.

Hector's head starts whistling the old sea shanty, "What Shall We Do With A Drunken Sailor?":

Put him in the guard room till he's sober
Put him in bed with the captain's daughter...

04

TURNS out those coastal lights are those of a humble Mexican "resort complex."

"Resort complex."

Feh. Mostly, it's just your typical roadside hotel with a beach-front view.

I pay cash. Then I buy some khaki pants, a couple of Hawaiian shirts and pair of black Wayfarers in the resort's gift shop—such as it is.

Dressed in my new togs, I look like Jack Lord on his day off from *Five-O*.

Back in our room, I check to make sure the alarm clock is off, take the phone off the hook, shove a chair under the door knob and Hector's head under the bed and I eat some room service eggs, toast and orange juice.

Then Hector and me sleep the sleep of the dead.

* * *

Exhausted, I hit the shower.

Seeing myself naked for the first time in seven days isn't a happy experience. I'm one long and scrawny bruise. I've always run to bone, but the prominence of my ribs is scaring even me. You could slice open envelopes with my cheekbones. My knife wound is starting to worry me again and my shoulder doesn't feel quite right … not dislocated exactly, but surely separated.

I check my belly. Those old wounds where the maguey spikes bored into me, they'll never go away.

The bullet wound in my right calf.

All my broken and poorly set fingers and toes.

And my goddamned lost eye.

Jesus Christ. I'm a fucking poet! How did I end up with the body of a middle-aged mercenary?

I dress and walk to the lobby. There I pick up a newspaper and read the literary section over breakfast.

The number one book in the land?

Love Story.

Dear God.

But Hemingway, nine years dead, has managed to come in at number three—*Islands In the Stream.* It's a book I remember Hector telling me he read in typescript in Cuba in 1959. His reviews of the manuscript were mixed. Hec said it suffered from Hemingway's "lack of aesthetic distance from himself." Back then, I didn't quite understand what Hector meant.

Graham Greene has made the list, too, and that isn't bad.

But Irwin fucking Shaw?

And two Rod McKuen poetry books: *In Someone's Shadow* and *Caught in the Quiet.*

Try to soldier on through that sad success.

The hotelier is one of those Mexicans who crossed the border to fight the Nazis in a U.S. unit. He is totally blind, but managing to kick my ass at chess. We share a bottle of Scotch and play three games.

No, put it this way: I lose three games. We are starting the fourth when the call comes through.

"It's for you, Mr. Fiske," the hotelier's wife says. She is a delightful, charming little woman who can't be an inch over four-eleven.

A "call" for *me*. That can't bode well.

Wary, I say, "Hello?"

"Hey, pardner!"

I know that voice, but I can't quite place it. Sounds a little drunk, but plenty affable.

"Clearly, I know where you are, pard'. So you can figure I know that because Pop and Grandpop know where you are … you follow?"

"George?" I say, "George W.?"

"Get out of there, *hombre*. Go now and you can have maybe thirty minutes' head start. But you gotta go now. Vamoose."

"Why warn me?"

"They need to be humbled. And stealing an American's head? That ain't right. Geronimo is one thing, but Lassiter? That's unacceptable. And you're pissing away your lead, jawing like this. I'm buckin' big horses, Fiske. Don't make it all for nothing—for either of us. Fuck Dad."

I hang up; settle up. My heart pounding, I gather my stuff and Hector and run across the street, looking over my shoulder for spies.

A few blocks north of the hotel, I hear a train whistle. I run to its sound.

There is a big old diesel hauling a long chain of freight cars. It seems to be bound west. I find an unsecured door on one of the boxcars, sling my stuff and Hector's head up and in, and then I vault in after them.

We have the boxcar to ourselves.

Then I wonder if railroads still pay to employ railroad bulls.

Panting, sweating, I sit back in that sweltering car, thinking of Woody Guthrie and Hector's and Hemingway's tales of hopping freights. Feels like I should have a harmonica or something.

Hector must feel the same way ... he is humming some song and mumbling its lyrics. Some tune called *something* "Mixteca."

05

MATAMOROS: against all odds, I made it here alive.

I hole up in a hotel room for three days, room service food and hotel papers and pens, collaborating on this new novel with Hector.

There is a knock at the door. A woman's voice that I know says, "Bud, it's me. It's Alicia."

Oh my God, look at her. She was always beautiful … and now she's handsome, too.

Her black hair is cut a bit shorter and she's lost some weight.

She hugs me hard, then half-turns.

Three children move into my room with her. One is older—her first daughter, I guess.

The other two, a bit younger, are twins—a girl and a boy.

I have no doubt about whom their father is.

It is so strange, so moving, to see Hector's blue eyes staring up at me from these dusky, little Spanish faces.

There is a younger man behind Alicia, too. He resembles her. She introduces him as her brother, Augustin.

"Take the children downstairs," she tells him. "I need to speak with Bud."

They leave and she comes and sits on the bed beside me. She takes my hands and rests them on her lap. "You look like hell, Bud. There have been many close calls?"

"Many," I say. "I'm clean for now, I think."

"You won't be for long. We somehow picked up a tail yesterday. Some bad people from back in New Mexico. Three brothers—triplets. Very, *very* bad. We've lost them for the moment, but they know we are in town. So we only have a few minutes, I'm afraid. I wish …"

Have to confess that I'm not sure where she is going with that.

I suddenly have the urge to kiss her, hard.

But Hector's memory hangs between us like a ghost.

And in actual fact, he is hiding under the bed.

"These men who will chase you, soon, the Castillo Brothers, they are very bad, and very focused."

"I understand."

"We came in two cars," she says. "Me and my brother and my children will leave in one. They have not identified that car with us yet." She reaches in her purse and hands me a set of keys. "These are to Héctor's old Chevy," she says. "You remember the car?"

"Sure." I loved that Bel Air: sucker *spanked*.

"They followed Augustin, who was driving that car," she says. "I suppose they knew following us would eventually get them to you, and therefore to Héctor." She shakes her head. "There's not even treasure to justify them wanting Héctor's head. It's all hubris—stupid pride. *Machismo*, I suppose."

"Sure," I say again.

"Héctor's car has a full tank of gas," she says, searching my remaining eye. "There are guns, loaded and ready, in the trunk and glove compartment. There is another head in the trunk—a decoy."

I'm tempted to ask whose head. Instead I say, "Don't be specific—it's better I don't know details—but once I get out there, and they come after me, vaguely, what will you do?"

"I need a day. That's all." She shakes her head. "'That's all.' That's like an eternity with those bastards who will be following you. But one day, if you can give us that day, will let us get to the plane we have chartered. We moved Héctor not long after the bastards took his head. We also exhumed his daughter, Dolores. We will bury them somewhere safe in the San Joaquin valley. In a good and secret place."

"The San Joaquin was Hector's favorite place," I remember. "He once told me it was the only place on earth he ever wanted to see twice."

She squeezes my hand, hard. "We have to do this soon. If they find Héctor's Chevy before you go …"

"Just tell me where to find it. You'll have your day."

"It's parked in the alley out back. Augustin has thrown a tarp over it."

I stand up and begin gathering my things. Hesitating, I say, "Your youngest children—they're his, aren't they?"

Alicia nods.

"Did he know?"

"Not at first. When he did … it was too late for any of us."

"They're beautiful."

She smiles and strokes my cheek.

I want to ask, "Are you happy? Happy out there without a man, living in Hector's old house?" I want to keep talking with her…

But I stroke her hair behind her ear and cup her chin. "It's good to see you a last time. Even like this."

She hugs me tightly and then kisses me hard on the mouth.

I reach under the bed and hand her the bag with Hector's head. She squeezes my arm with fierce pressure. "You run hard and fast now, Bud. Don't let them get you. Then one day, a day soon, I hope, you'll come to New Mexico and stay with us. You can tell the children stories about their father."

"Sure. There's nothing I'd love more than that."

We hug a last time and then she is gone.

Dazed, I wander to the mirror—rub the remnants of her lipstick from the side of my mouth. I can taste her lips. I wash my face a last time, call downstairs and ask that a large travel cup of black coffee be made ready for me. Then I pull on my boots.

The tarp comes off easily and I cast it onto the street. I pop the trunk and look at the bag with the phony head. There is a Magnum in the trunk, too. Big, wicked looking thing. I take the gun out and close the trunk on the stranger's head.

The engine turns on the first try—the Bel Air has been well cared for in the intervening thirteen years. I push down the button to release the top—make it easier for those cocksucker triplets to spot me. Then I pull out on the streets and drive around town slow for a time, the radio turned up to blasting.

Within a half-an-hour, I know that I have been spotted by those wicked triplets.

They are driving a blue Charger: three skinny, dark-faced men with long, black hair.

Only their individual scars—many, many of these—set their faces apart from one another.

Spooked, I run three red lights just to avoid being stopped in traffic where they might lay hands on me.

When we hit the outskirts of town, I put my foot to the firewall.

Three hours in, Hector says to me, "You realize the math just isn't on our side, Bud."

I look over at him. He's sitting there, the wind pushing around his hair, his elbow on the window. This sad smile. I say, "Explain."

He shrugs. "Three of them, Bud. One of you. Well, only you, because I can't drive anymore. First time you stop to fill the tank, they'll probably move on you. But even if they don't, they can sleep in shifts. You can't. Any way you slice it, they're foreordained to win this race."

Hector is right. *Again.*

If I were one of those Tarahumara Indians Hector's talked about, I might withstand the tyranny of the math. But I'm not.

And I started this chase already beaten down by a week of running. So I say, "Any ideas?"

"No good ones," Hector replies, tossing a Pall Mall out the window. "If I could still do it, I'd slide over into the backseat and cut a hole through to the trunk. Grab me one of those Tommy guns and strafe those bastards as you hit the brakes to bring 'em closer."

Then I remember that long-ago day in downtown Los Angeles, when Hector played chicken with Rodolfo Fierro and his friends. I check the mirror. There's a cloud of dust, perhaps a mile back. I slow and palm the wheel, belling out in a big curve and heading back the way we've just come, foot pushing the pedal to the floor.

I reach for the Magnum.

Steering with my right hand, I extend my left out the window, the butt of the gun braced on the rearview mirror.

At this speed, and pointed at one another, it's going to be dicey. But if I succeed in shooting the driver before he shoots me or actually rams our Chevy, well, the rest should take care of itself.

I glance over a last time.

Hector smiles and winks back at me.

Above the roar of the wind sheer, Hector hollers, "If we survive this Bud—if you take those cocksuckers out—well, then I've got a hankering to head into the high country. What do you say we go find those Tarahumara Indians? See if we can't figure out what makes those bastards run like they do."

Les ruego que me perdonen
Si al narrar meti la pata
Pero asi cuentan murio
Don Francisco Villa.

—Anonymous

ACKNOWLEDGEMENTS

I am indebted to Svetlana Pironko, Michael O'Brien and Ben LeRoy for their support and belief in this novel. I'm also grateful to Alison Janssen for her superb edit and suggestions.

Special thanks also to Debbie, Madeleine and Yeats McDonald.

Head Games is a work of fiction rooted in historical fact. As such, it draws on contemporary newspaper accounts regarding the theft of Pancho Villa's head and the arrests that followed that crime. The whereabouts of Villa's head actually became a campaign issue during the U.S. presidential race between George Herbert Walker Bush and Michael Dukakis. Some within the Mexican government continue to press George W. Bush to use his status as a Skull and Bones member to return the missing skull.

Two books were of particular use in the writing of this novel. The first is a biography of Emil Holmdahl entitled *Soldier of Fortune*, by Douglas V. Meed (Halcyon Press LTD, 2003). The second is *Character Studies: Encounters with the Curiously Obsessed*, by Mark Singer (Houghton Mifflin Company, 2005) which contains a chapter on Pancho Villa's missing skull and those in Texas still obsessed with its return. *Dangerous Friends*, by Peter Viertel (Doubleday, 1992), also provided useful information about Ernest Hemingway and Orson Welles.